PERFECT

As a professional storyteller, **Cathy Miyata** performs on stages across Ontario and around the world. She loves stories and has been writing them down since she was a young girl. Cathy is inspired by the funny things that happen to her — she writes them down in her "ho ho journal" and uses them in her work.

Cathy and her family live in Burlington, Ontario. This is her first novel.

"Good for you!" he said, and patted my shoulder again. "Now, we'd better get going." Slowly, we walked across the stage. At the top of the stairs he stopped and looked down at me.

"You should know, though, directing is not what you're best at."

"Oh?" I looked at him uneasily. "What am I best at?"

Mr. Cowles smiled broadly. "Being a friend, Ashley. You're *definitely* the best at that."

I imagined Krystal on stage singing "Somewhere over the Rainbow" and everyone clapping and clapping. I smiled my best smile. I felt like a shiny star.

All at once, the noise from the audience seemed to fill the whole backstage. Mr. Cowles held out his elbow and I looped my arm through his.

"It's showtime!" I boomed in my best director's voice and we marched down the stairs together.

PERFECT
NATASHA FRIEND

SCHOLASTIC INC.

New York Toronto London Auckland Sydney
Mexico City New Delhi Hong Kong Buenos Aires

ISBN 0-439-90013-1

Text copyright © 2004 by Natasha Friend. All rights reserved. Published by Scholastic Inc., 557 Broadway, New York, NY 10012, by arrangement with Milkweed Editions. SCHOLASTIC and associated logos are trademarks and/or registered trademarks of Scholastic Inc.

12 11 10 9 8 7 6 5 4 3 2 1   6 7 8 9 10 11/0

Printed in the U.S.A.   40

First Scholastic printing, September 2006

Cover and interior design by Christian Fünfhausen

Cover and interior images by Jarrod Riddle

The text of this book is set in Goudy Old Style.

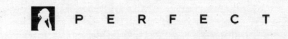

PERFECT

1

APRIL USED TO BE MY SISTER. She used to be nine and charming. She used to respect the two most important laws of sisterhood: *Thou shalt not spy* and *Thou shalt not report thy sister's crimes to the authorities.*

Now Ape Face is ten and everything's different. She is evil, and she must be destroyed.

Here's how it happened: The week before school started, my ex-sister burst through the closed door of the bathroom we share and found me. On my knees. With my head in the toilet.

"Euwww," she said. "Naaasty."

I removed my fingers from my throat and swallowed. "Don't tell Mom."

"Don't tell Mom what?" she said.

"That I have the *flu*, April. Obviously. I don't want her to worry."

"Ohhh. Is *that* what it is? The *flu?*"

I wanted to call her the worst name I could think of—something I heard Jason Gullo call Ryan James in gym. But with Ape Face, you have to choose your words carefully. "You'd better not tell her."

Ape Face raised one eyebrow. "Or what?"

"Or else. That's all I'm saying."

"Oooo." She waggled her fingers at me. "*Scary.*"

Here is our business arrangement in times of crisis: bribery. Of the items I own, here is what April wants: everything.

We stepped into my office, which doubles as a bedroom, and shut the door. As if shutting doors means anything around here.

"My rhinestone barrettes," I said.

Ape Face wrinkled her nose. She has no taste. She wears a leotard to school, if that tells you anything. And anyway, just as a good batter never swings at the first pitch, Ape Face never takes the first offer. She likes me to throw some heat.

I went over to my bureau and pulled out my pink tank top. There was a time when Ape Face would have gnawed off her own arm for this shirt. That is, before there was a gigantic ravioli stain on the front.

"Right," said Ape Face, and made a move toward the door.

I had to say something. Anything. "My Wonderbra?"

Ape Face said, "That's very funny, Isabelle. You should be a comedian."

"I'm serious. It makes you look like you have something on top even when you don't."

Ape Face narrowed her eyes at me. "Do you know that you are exactly ten seconds away from being grounded for life?"

I couldn't tell if she was trying to scare me or if she meant it. With three balls, no strikes, I couldn't take the chance. This one was gonna hurt. "My red boots," I said. *Ouch*.

"The suede ones?" said Ape Face, brightening.

"The suede ones." Noooooooo. These are my absolute favorite boots in the whole world and she knows it. I saved my allowance for three months to buy them.

Regret! Regret!

Ape Face came over to my bed and sat down, one leg crossed over the other. She held out her hand to me like she was royalty and I was supposed to kiss her ring.

I reached under the bed to get the shoe box and handed it to her.

Ape Face took her sweet time. She laced up each boot with excruciating care. She pointed her toes in the air, flexed. Pointed, flexed, assumed ballet positions. She stood and did a few pliés and arabesques. Then, even more slowly, she sat back down and unlaced. Slowly, oh so slowly, she placed my all-time favorite boots back in their tissue paper cocoon.

She handed me the box. "I don't think so, Isabelle. They're a little scuffed."

She's that good.

"Okay, April. Name it."

"Your mountain bike." She actually said this with a straight face.

"You're crazy."

"Your mountain bike," she repeated.

"Have you been sniffing glue? Those fumes, you know, they can make you nuts."

Ape Face walked over to the door, placed one hand on the doorknob. "This is my final offer, Belly. Take it or . . . don't."

I have never hated anyone so much in my entire life as I hated my sister at that moment. "Get out of my room," I told her. "*Out.*"

"Have it your way," Ape Face said. And here is what she, my own flesh and blood, did: she placed both hands on her nonhips, smiled at me, and started yelling. "Mahh-hhhm! Belly's puking her guts out!"

That's how it happened. That's how my ex-sister realized her lifelong dream of seeing me placed under house arrest. That's how I ended up here, on this pee-colored couch from the disco era, sandwiched between a skeleton and a whale.

2

"GROUP" IS MY PUNISHMENT. As in "Eating Disorder and Body Image Therapy Group." It is just how you wish you could spend every day for the rest of your life: sitting around in a circle, talking about things you don't want to talk about, in a room with no air circulation and orange carpet that smells like Cheez-Its.

The first day of Group I wouldn't get out of the car. My mother had us parked in a ten-minute spot, but that didn't make me move any faster. I stared out the window at absolutely nothing. Then I fiddled with the radio. When I'm in the mood I can switch stations so fast you can't even tell what song is playing. It is quite a talent.

Finally my mother reached over and turned it off.

"What?" I said. "I was listening."

"Isabelle." She put her hand on my arm. "It's almost five. You don't want to be late."

I moved as far away from her hand as I could get. "Yes, I do," I said. "I want to be very, very late. You have no idea how late I want to be."

My mother sighed and gripped the steering wheel with both hands.

I turned the radio on again and fiddled with the buttons like crazy, which you would think would make a mother furious. Not this mother. She is the type that says, in a voice so gentle you want to scream, "Oh, honey."

"Fine!" I turned off the radio. I unbuckled my seat belt to make her think I was planning on going somewhere. "Just answer me one thing. Why are you making me do this?"

"Because that is the deal," my mother said.

"Some deal. It's not like I had a choice."

"You're right." My mother took off the stupid black sunglasses she always has to wear when she goes out, even when it's raining. She turned to look at me. "About this, you don't have a choice. You need to do this one thing."

Now I was the one who reached over to touch her arm. "Mom. Please? It was just that one time I threw up. I won't do it again. I promise."

"I know you won't," she said.

"You do?"

"Yes."

"So I don't have to go?"

"No," Mom said, shaking her head slowly. "You do have to go. That's how I know you won't do it again."

"Huh," I said. I made my voice quiet and spoke directly to the windshield. The worst words possible. "Daddy would never make me go. Not in a million years."

The silence was so big it made my stomach ache.

My mother couldn't look at me. "I'll pick you up at six thirty," she said in a wobbly voice. On went the sunglasses.

When I got out of the car I slammed the door as hard as I could. I didn't care if she cried. She could cry all day if she wanted to. Just for once, though, I'd like her to do it out in the open, not hiding behind something like sunglasses. It's a wonder she doesn't go blind.

I stood at the curb, watching my mother fumble with the car keys for about a hundred years until she finally turned on the ignition. I figured I might as well wait until she pulled away, so she could wave good-bye to me like everything was fine. And I could wave back like nothing had happened.

The leader of Group is Trish, who has hair like Orphan Annie and an overbite. I know what an overbite is only because I have one too. At least I used to, before I got braces. Now all I have is a mouth full of metal.

The first day, Trish bounced around handing out three-by-five cards and touching everyone on the shoulder. "Here you go. . . . Here you go. . . ." She's the camp counselor type. If anyone can make a rope ladder out of dental floss, it's Trish.

"Welcome to Group!" Trish said. "Why don't we go

around the room and introduce ourselves. . . . Mathilde?" Trish pounced on the girl to my left. "Would you like to start?"

When Mathilde ducked her head, you could see all five of her chins. I'm not saying this to be mean, it really happened. She spoke so softly we could barely hear her. "I'm . . . uh . . . Mathilde."

"Great!" said Trish. "Hi, Mathilde. Let's all say 'Hiii, Mathilde.'"

We all said, "Hiii, Mathilde."

You have to feel badly for Mathilde. You really do. First of all, she wears things like shorts with little strawberries on them, and T-shirts with iron-on kittens. You can bet her grandmother picks them out. Second, she has the fattest legs I've ever seen. Next to hers, my legs look like sticks.

"Dawn?" said Trish.

"I'm Dawn," said Dawn, the cute girl sitting across from me. Long yellow bangs, sad eyes, pug nose. I liked her right away.

"Hiii, Dawn," we said.

Then there was Rachel. Rachel looks like she should be in a gang. She has about ten earrings in each ear and black eyeliner all around her eyes. You can guess what she's thinking just from looking at her. *I don't need you people! I don't need anyone!*

"Hiii, Rachel," we said anyway.

Next was Lila, who is superskinny. She's always tapping her fingertips against her kneecaps. Her skin is white, white, white, and you can count her ribs through her turtleneck.

Most people would probably think that's gross, being able to count someone's ribs through their shirt, but personally, I wouldn't mind looking like Lila. It's better than being fat. Way better.

"Hiii, Lila," we said.

Finally there was me. Isabelle Lee. Here's the problem with Isabelle Lee: shorten it, and what do you get? Izzy Lee, which I hate. Or Belle Lee, which is just as bad. And Belly? Well, Belly is unforgivable. I wake up every day ready to kill Ape Face for coming up with that one.

I used to be Bella, Daddy's name for me. But then he died and I wouldn't let anyone call me that anymore. If they did I'd bite their head right off.

Nobody in Group knows about that. To them, I'm just Isabelle, and that's how it's going to stay.

"Hiii, Isabelle."

"Hi," I said. My voice came out so squeaky I didn't even recognize it.

Trish looked at her watch and said we should wait a few more minutes, there were supposed to be six of us. Right on cue, someone knocked at the door.

Trish said, "Come on in, Ashley."

And in she walked: Ashley Barnum. *The* Ashley Barnum.

I could not have been more surprised if I woke up to find my head stapled to my pillow. I was so dumbfounded I had to mouth the words. *Hiii, Ashley.*

Here is what you have to know about Ashley Barnum to understand: First of all, the name. *Ashley Barnum.* Royalty, right? When Ashley Barnum walks down the hall at school, you know it, and not just by the hundreds of wanna-be Ashleys who follow her everywhere. By her glow. For starters, she has blue eyes, surfer-girl hair, and perfect thighs—skinny, but muscular too, the kind that flex instead of jiggle. You can bet they don't rub together when she walks.

On top of that, she is captain of the field hockey team and vice president of the eighth grade. Last year she was voted most popular girl, and everybody knows that when we get to high school she'll be homecoming queen and prom queen and every other kind of queen. Let's face it, Ashley Barnum is the type of girl that, if she stepped in dog doo, every guy would line up for the honor of licking her feet clean. Not that dogs would dare doo in Ashley Barnum's path. Even they would rather die.

Ashley has three brothers, high-school age. They all look like male versions of Ashley. Craig, Jonathan, and David are their names, and they take turns driving her to school in a silver convertible, so she doesn't have to take the bus like the rest of us. They are her bodyguards. One Barbie, three Kens.

Once, I thought I could hate Ashley Barnum on account of her being so perfect all the time, but here is the clincher, here is the real tragedy: she's nice. At least if she were a snob I could be left in peace.

This year, we have the same English class, Advanced with Mr. Minx. Now that we're in eighth grade, everything is split into ability levels: basic, standard, and advanced. I'm in all advanced. I'm pretty good at everything, except for math. At math I'm the pits.

In Mr. Minx's English class, Ashley Barnum sits front and center. Dan Fosse and Peter Marsh, soccer players (drool), sit on Ashley's right and left, only too happy to play the bread to her peanut butter. Like every other guy in the school, they spend each fifty-minute period waiting for Ashley to sneeze so they can bless her.

Brian King sits behind her. He is in love with her. Everyone knows that ol' Bri is not exactly in Ashley Barnum's league. He's doughy, and there's always dirt under his fingernails, and he wears these thick glasses that are constantly sliding halfway down his nose. But does that stop him from writing love notes and dropping them onto her desk on his way to the pencil sharpener? Nope. He's been doing this since sixth grade. And Ashley always smiles and says thank you. She slips Brian's notes into her backpack like she's going to read them later. Why? Because she's nice.

I sit in the back row, between Nola Quentin and Georgine Miner, my friends since kindergarten. I like Nola and Georgie all right, but let's just say that they are not going to win any beauty contests. No boy would think to pass a note to either one of them. Or to me.

But Ashley Barnum? Well, she is the kind of person you wish you could be friends with, even though she doesn't know you exist. When I was younger I even wanted to be her, so much that I used to doodle her name all over my desk. Instead of your regular doodles—rainbows (R.O.Y.G.B.I.V.), hearts (true love always), and cubes (3-D), my doodle was Ashley Barnum (bubble letters).

So when she walked into Group that day, you can

imagine my shock. Here was Ashley Barnum, wearing a jean miniskirt and matching clogs. Her eyes were pink, but other than that she was her usual radiant self. Obviously she'd stumbled upon our meeting by mistake. Someone should have told her that the meeting for "People without a Care in the World" was one floor down.

Trish put her arm around Ashley's shoulder and squeezed. She handed Ashley a three-by-five card and guided her to a chair.

"The information you share on these cards, girls," Trish said, "is private. The first rule of Group is confidentiality. That means that anything that's shared in this room *stays* in this room."

Trish stood next to an easel draped with grainy paper. "Pretend this is your card," she said. With red marker, Trish drew six big dots. She wanted our full name, the name we prefer to be called, age, grade in school, reason for coming to Group, and a few of our personal goals.

"This part is important," said Trish, double-underlining "personal goals." "What kind of person do you want to be when you leave Group today? A month from now? A year?"

Trish walked around passing out golf pencils.

"Could I possibly have something less stubby?" said Rachel, like she'd just been handed a used Kleenex.

"Certainly." Trish smiled and handed her a Bic instead. "Anyone else prefer a pen?"

The rest of us murmured "No, thank you" and went to work on our three-by-fives.

When I finished, mine looked like this:

My name is: Isabelle Eliza Lee
Please call me: Isabelle
I am: 13 yrs. old
I am in: 8th
I am here b/c: that was "the deal"
My personal goal is: ???

I leaned a little to the left and tried to sneak a peek at Mathilde's card. All I could make out were the words *fat pig*, before she flipped it over. Lila was hunched over hers like it was a vocabulary quiz and we were all trying to cheat off her. Ashley Barnum was sitting directly across the room from me, bending sideways over Trish's desk. A curtain of blonde hair fell across her face.

I imagined her card to read:

- MY NAME IS: Ashley Joy Barnum.
- PLEASE CALL ME: Ashley.
- I AM: thirteen years old.
- I AM IN: the eighth grade.
- I AM HERE BECAUSE: I want to help make the world a better place. For my extra-credit Advanced Science project I have gone undercover to research the two most horrible diseases facing young girls today: bulimia and anorexia. I feel that as a future *Seventeen* cover model and pediatrician, I would

be an irresponsible citizen if I didn't learn as
much as I possibly can about the impact of eating
disorders on the bodies, minds, and emotions of
eighth-grade girls.
• MY PERSONAL GOAL IS: to get an A++ on my
project, to be an eating and exercise role model
for the Group, and to help make the world a little
brighter in the process.

Trish collected our cards and told us how proud she
was of us already.

"Have a restful week," Trish said. "Be good to your-
selves." She reminded us to bring a blank book to next
Wednesday's Group, for journaling purposes.

Ten minutes later, we were standing outside the hospital,
waiting for the moms to pick us up. Me and Ashley Barnum. Ashley Barnum and Me. She was drawing swirls in
the dirt with one toe. I was doing standing butt crunches.
One-and-two-and-three-and-four-and . . . I was on number
seventy-nine when she said, "Isabelle?"

"Yes?" I couldn't believe it. She was speaking to me.
Ashley Barnum was actually speaking to me.

"You go to John Jay, right?"

"Yes."

"8-A homeroom?"

"Yes."

"Minx's English?"

"Why, yes." *Why, yes?* Suddenly I'd developed a British accent? Duh!

"Well, here's the thing," Ashley said. "I mean . . . I know we don't really know each other or anything, but I'd really appreciate it if you wouldn't, you know . . ."

"I won't tell," I said.

Ashley Barnum drew another snail trail in the dirt, nodded. "Thanks."

"Sure."

"Anyway," Ashley said, "it's not a big deal or anything. I mean, my mom just flipped about this gum she found in my backpack. She thought it was, um, Ex-Lax or some-thing? She saw this thing on TV . . ."

"Yeah," I said. "Same. I mean, my mom flipped too, 'cause she thought I was throwing up or something."

"Yeah?" said Ashley Barnum.

"Yeah."

There was a pause while I tried to think of something cool to say. *Do you know I've wanted to be you since fourth grade?*

But Ashley's mom pulled up in her shiny black car and signaled with her cigarette for Ashley to hurry up, and Ashley said, superfast, "So, thanks, Isabelle. I'll see you in Minx's class, third period, 'kay!"

"'Kay," I said. "Minx's class." *You betcha, girlfriend. Call ya later!*

As the car peeled out, a little spray of dirt fanned through the air, just above the spot where Ashley Barnum's toe had been.

3

THAT NIGHT I MADE IT THROUGH an entire dinner without talking to Ape Face. I wanted to drive her bonkers.

"If you think the silent treatment bothers me," she said, "think again."

"Mom?" I said. "Would you pass the peas, please?"

"You can ask your sister for the peas, Isabelle. They're right in front of her."

My mother had about six peas on her plate, and a

piece of chicken the size of her thumb. This is how much she eats. Before Daddy, she ate real people's meals. Now she eats doll meals.

Ape Face held up the bowl, balancing it on one hand. "Would anyone like some peas? . . . Anyone?"

"So, Mom," I said, completely ignoring Ape Face. "How was your day? Any exciting papers to grade?"

My mother is a college professor. She teaches American literature. There are piles of her students' papers all over the house. People say, "Wow, your mother's pretty messy." But they don't know she used to be neat.

"Isabelle," my mother said. "April is offering you the peas."

"I changed my mind," I said. "I'm not in the mood for peas after all."

"Honestly, Isabelle," said my mother.

"Honestly, Isabelle," said Ape Face, frowning and shaking her head.

My mother shot April the look that means *Enough*.

"Mom, do you hear anything?" I asked. "I don't hear anything. . . . What's that? . . . Is that a fly buzzing in my ear?"

"Isabelle," said my mother quietly, spearing exactly one pea with her fork. "Stop it."

"Fine," I said.

There was a moment of silence. Then Ape Face said, "Mom, guess what? I'm writing a story. 'Group of Frogs,' it's called. How's that for a title?"

Mom reached over to ruffle the Ape's hair. "An excellent title. I can't wait to read it. What's the plot?"

This is the way it goes with them. They are their own mother-daughter book club. If you want to join, go right ahead.

I got up to clear my plate. On my way to the sink I did what I always do: try not to look at Daddy's empty chair, but can't help myself. This time there was a big, messy pile of papers on top of it. I couldn't believe it. A lot of people put piles of stuff on chairs and pass right by them, not thinking a thing. But looking at this pile, my stomach hurt so much I felt like someone punched me.

In my room, I ran straight to my closet. That's where I keep my stash, under one of Daddy's old flannel shirts that nobody knows I have. For the longest time after he died, I kept the shirt under my bed, wrapped in a paper bag. I would take it out whenever I missed him because it had his smell. Clean and warm, like grass.

This shirt was a legend. My mother was always trying to throw it out because of the missing buttons and the pocket that got ripped off in a football game. But every time Mom tried to get rid of the shirt, Daddy would rescue it just in time. It was their special game. *"There you are,"* he would say, dragging it out of the Goodwill bag and slipping it back on. And Mom would wag her finger at him, pretending to be angry. "Jacob Lee. You are impossible." This was his cue to chase her all around the house until he caught her and wrapped her up in his arms, in that big soft shirt that smelled like him.

One time last year, right before my birthday, I took the shirt out from under my bed and jammed my face in it, hard, because I missed him so much. That's when I realized it was all smelled out. I breathed in, and . . . nothing. It was just a shirt. Just a ratty old shirt that could have belonged to anyone.

There wasn't much left in my stash, only a few packages of Fig Newtons and a half-eaten bag of Doritos. I didn't bother pushing the bureau against the door this time because I knew Mom and Ape Face wouldn't be up for a while.

I sat on the floor of my closet while I ate, breathing in that mothbally closet smell. One hand on the Fig Newtons, the other on the chips. When I was finished, I put the empty wrappers back in the box and the box back on the top shelf of the closet, under the flannel shirt.

Before going to the bathroom I stood at the top of the stairs and listened. I could hear Mom and Ape Face laughing together. Who knew "Group of Frogs" was a freaking comedy?

In the bathroom I drank a glass of water as fast as I could. I lifted the toilet seat and stuck my fingers down my throat, so far down my middle knuckle was touching that little wiggly piece in the back. I felt my stomach contract hard and my shoulders hunch up to my ears. Abracadabra, out came the Doritos, the Fig Newtons, the milk, the pasta, the chicken cacciatore.

Just like magic.

Later, my mother knocked on the door. "Isabelle? May I come in?"

"It's a free country," I said. I was lying in bed with A

Separate Peace, this book we're reading for English.

"A *Separate Peace?*" Mom said. "That's one of my favorites. Have you gotten to the part where Finny shows Gene the tree?"

"I'm only on chapter one," I said.

"Oh. Well, I didn't ruin anything for you by telling you that. But the tree does become an important symbol in the novel. Let me know when you get there, and we can discuss it."

"Uh-huh." I picked the book back up and pretended to be very busy reading.

"Isabelle." My mother sat down on the edge of the bed and took the book right out of my hand.

"I'm reading!"

"Well, I'm talking."

I looked at the ceiling with my eyeballs. My mother could talk all night and still not say a thing.

She reached out to grab a loose thread hanging from my pajama sleeve. She twisted the thread around her finger, yanked. "So. How was it today?"

"How was what?"

"Group therapy."

"It's called Group, Mom."

"Okay. How was Group?"

"Fine."

"Did you find it helpful?"

"Not particularly."

"Well, give it some time."

I didn't say anything. I just kept looking at the ceiling, thinking about my stash in the closet, how it was getting low.

I felt my mother shifting on the bed. I knew she wanted me to tell her I was fine. In her head she was probably saying, *How did I get one normal daughter and one screwup?*

Well, guess what your screwup was doing while you were downstairs planning Ape Face's fabulous writing career?

"I need a blank book," I said. "You know, a journal. For next Wednesday."

"Oh?" said my mother. I could hear a little smile in her voice. "You'll be writing in Group? Great! We'll pick one up this weekend."

Yippee.

I felt her look at me, then away, then at me again.

"What?" I said.

"Nothing."

"*What?*"

"Nothing, Isabelle," she said. "It's just . . . well, lots of girls your age begin worrying about their weight. When in fact it's natural that their bodies start carrying extra fat."

"Whatever," I said. It gave me the creeps the way she said that. *Carrying extra fat.* Like I had a backpack full of butter instead of books.

"Anyway," Mom continued, "if you're worried about it, how about trying to eat more fruits and veggies? Less junk? We could probably all do to cut back on our calories around here, eat some healthier meals." She patted her stomach and smiled. "Your mother included."

I looked at her, raised an eyebrow.

"There are much less dangerous ways to lose weight than making yourself throw up, Isabelle. How does that sound? We could do it together. Okay?"

I knew she wanted me to say okay more than anything. It didn't even matter if the okay was a lie.

I didn't say anything.

"Isabelle? Please. I want to help."

"Um . . . ," I said, like I was thinking it over. "Sure."

"Great! I'll do the grocery shopping tomorrow. I'll go to Whole Foods, even."

"Great," I said, feeling terrible.

When she leaned over to kiss me goodnight I held my breath. Even though I'd brushed my teeth twice and rinsed with mouthwash, I didn't want her to smell what I'd done.

In the middle of the night, I woke up and couldn't go back to sleep. This happens a lot but it's worst when I can hear Mom. Most of the time I just put my pillow over my head and hum for a while to drown her out. This time I went and stood in the hallway outside her bedroom. The light from the crack under the door made a long, skinny rectangle on the wood floor, covering the tips of my toes.

She was crying. Not loud, but loud enough. And she was saying his name, over and over again, the way she always does when she thinks we can't hear her. *Jay. Oh, Jacob. Oh, Jay.*

I waited outside the door for her to stop crying. But she didn't.

"Mom?" I whispered. "Mommy? . . . Are you okay?"

She didn't answer, but I know she heard me. I know because the light went out right away, and everything was silent.

"Mom?"

I waited a while longer. I waited even though I knew she wouldn't answer, no matter how long I stood there.

Finally I left. I didn't even try to be quiet. I didn't tiptoe, I walked like a normal person down the hall, down the stairs, across the living room to the kitchen, and across the kitchen to the refrigerator.

Bread and butter, pasta salad, string cheese, strawberry yogurt, applesauce, more bread and butter, cold leftover pizza, olives, peanut butter straight out of the jar. I ate until my cheeks hurt, until the skin of my belly was stretched tight like a drum. Then I opened a brand-new carton of orange juice and drank the entire thing, standing up. Orange juice ran down my chin and onto the front of my nightgown. It dripped onto my bare feet. Every swallow hurt, but I didn't care. After a while, it almost feels good, the hurting.

The first time it happened was the day of Daddy's funeral. Our house was full of strangers, all of them patting my head, talking in whispers. Every so often my mother would come over to me and April and squeeze the breath out of us with her hugs. "Don't cry," she kept saying. "We will none of us cry." Finally some lady I didn't know came up to me with a plate and said, "Here you go, honey. Try to eat a little something." So I did. I ate cold cuts and salads and fancy cookies. I ate a whole pile of brownies. Whatever I wanted I ate. I ate until it hurt to stand up. Finally I went into the bathroom and puked three times.

The first time is hard because you don't know what you're doing. Now, in the middle of the night, it's simple.

I stood over the kitchen sink with my fingers down my throat, watching everything come back up. Afterward I went over to Daddy's old chair. I picked up the big pile of papers sitting there. I walked them into my mother's study and dropped them on top of her desk, where they belonged.

But I didn't cry. Not once.

4

MR. MINX'S CLASS, THURSDAY. Ashley Barnum didn't speak to me.

It's not that I expected she'd sit with me or anything. It's not like I thought we'd be best buds now, just because we talked for two minutes. Still, did she or did she not say "See you in Minx's class third period"?

Minx's class, Friday. Not a peep.

Maybe the word *see* meant just that. She would see me, but not necessarily speak to me. In which case, fine, she was off the hook.

Minx's class, Monday. Nothing.

Quite possibly, Ashley Barnum was ignoring me on purpose. And could I blame her? Get caught talking to a loser like me, and the popularity rug could be yanked out from under you like that. Poof!

Minx's class is bad enough as it is. It is the kind of class where you scrunch down in your seat the whole time, praying you don't get called on. What Mr. Minx loves is books. What he loves even more is the sound of his own voice. Sometimes, when he's reading out loud, he gets so impressed with himself you can actually see tears in his eyes. On Tuesday, he was as gaga as ever.

"Vocabulary dictation," said Minx, holding a stump of yellow chalk to his mouth and tapping his upper lip with it. "Adjectives. . . . Alienated. Disenchanted. Disillusioned."

Another thing about Minx, he loves using big words. Those three he said, I had no idea what they meant. Minx knew it too. "I'm getting some blank looks, people. If you don't know a word, get out your dictionary. This is Advanced English. *Advanced.* You are expected to take some initiative here."

Minx squinted across the room, holding the chalk stump in the air like a dart. "Alienated . . . Disenchanted . . . Disillusioned . . ."

He gave us about ten seconds with our dictionaries before he fired a question at us. "When . . . under what circumstances . . . might one feel *alienated?* Hmm?"

Minx paced the aisles in his Wal-Mart sneakers, the Velcro kind. He stopped at the end of my row and pivoted, tapping Georgine's desk with his chalk. "I'm not asking this question for my health, people." *Taptaptaptap.* "I'm actually looking for an intelligent response. Ms. Miner, do you have an intelligent response?"

Georgie sank a little lower in her seat. She shook her head no.

Minx gave her desk one final tap and moved on to the next row. As soon as he was out of earshot Georgie leaned over and poked me with her pen. "Alienated, like *alien?*" she whispered.

I shrugged back.

Georgie is what you would call a worrier. She worries like crazy when she doesn't know the right answer for something. You can tell she's stressing by these two little lines between her eyes. Every so often she gets one of her "tension headaches," as her mother calls them, and has to stay home from school for two days without any visitors. Georgie's mother is very bugsome, to tell you the truth. If I had to live with her I'd get tension headaches too.

In Minx's class you have to watch him every second. You never know when he's going to pounce. It's best to take certain precautions. Like for instance, you wouldn't want to be reading a comic book.

"Mr. Fosse," Minx said, leaning over Dan Fosse's desk and snatching *Spider-Man* right out of his hands. "If you would be so kind as to beam the great light of your knowledge upon us."

Dan Fosse looked up at Minx. "Huh?"

"Huh?" said Minx. "Earth to Mr. Fosse. Come in, Mr. Fosse. We are discussing adjectives, which, as you may recall, are those pesky parts of speech that describe things. Words like *Inattentive. Oblivious. Negligent.*"

"Sorry," Dan muttered.

"As am I," said Minx, not sounding one bit sorry.

Minx may think he's the coolest thing on the planet, but here's something most people don't know. I saw him outside of school once, on a Saturday night. April and I were walking into Movie Mayhem and he was walking out, wearing the exact same getup he wears to school: white shirt with yellow armpit stains and tan corduroys. He even had one of those fluorescent bands strapped to his calf, to keep his pant cuff out of his bike chain. I reached across the metal divider and waved my hand in front of his face. "Hi, Mr. Minx. It's me, Isabelle Lee." Minx blinked at me a few times, like a mole. "Oh. Hello there, Ms. Lee," he said, and he hightailed it out of there, but not before I saw the movie he'd picked out: *The Parent Trap*.

The Parent Trap!

Minx scuttled over to Ashley's desk, opened his palms to Heaven. "Ms. Barnum. Please."

Ashley tucked a piece of hair behind her ear and clicked her ballpoint pen a few times. "I think," she said slowly, "that I would feel *a*lienated if . . . if I traveled to another country. Like Zimbabwe, for instance? And I didn't know the language, or the customs. And I didn't have the right clothes. . . . That would also be, um, a disenchanting experience."

A disenchanting experience? Come on. Sometimes Ashley Barnum sounds like she is trying out for the part of the thesaurus in the school play.

Minx bobbed his head up and down like a puppet. "Yes. Yesss. Excellent, Ms. Barnum. Excellent."

Ashley smiled and clicked her pen a few more times. She is so used to being right.

Brian King was practically falling out of his chair, he was so in love with her right then. He was probably composing another love note in his head that very second. *Dear Ashley, My love for you is not alienating, or a disenchanting experience. Oh, no, my darling. It is like . . . it is like . . .*

Minx walked back over to Dan Fosse's seat, picked up Dan's dictionary, and whacked it against the edge of the desk. *Wham!* "You see, people?" *Wham! Wham!* "It helps to actually *look* the words *up*. The dictionary is your *friend*."

Apparently Mr. Minx is in the habit of whacking his friends against his desk.

On and on he went. "There are still a few spots open in Standard English. I believe there are also a few in Basic English. Any takers?"

This, coming from a grown man who rents *The Parent Trap*. I wanted to climb up on my desk and announce to the world that our English teacher—the one who thinks he's the Albert Einstein of books—rents eight-year-old girl movies in his spare time.

The problem is I have no guts. I had to wait until I was outside the classroom to open my mouth. "Minx is a total jerk."

It was then that Ashley Barnum, with one hand on the water fountain and the other holding back a bunch of blonde hair, turned to stare at me. She licked a bead of water from her upper lip and said, in this very deep voice, "I believe there are a few spots open in Standard English, Ms. Lee."

I wagged my finger at her. "And several in Basic English, Ms. Barnum."

Ashley tossed her hair over one shoulder. She crossed her eyes and smiled at the same time.

As I was walking down the hall toward my locker, it occurred to me that Ashley Barnum and I had just shared A Moment.

At lunch, I sat with Nola and Georgine as usual. This new girl, Paula Harbinger from Cleveland, sat with us. Given the choice Paula would probably rather sit at a different table. With the cheerleaders, for instance. Or with the soccer team girls. But you can't just sit anywhere you want in the cafeteria. You have to get asked to sit at certain tables.

"Is that all you're eating?" Paula asked when I pulled out my lunch. Two hard-boiled eggs and some carrot sticks.

I shrugged. "I don't really like lunch."

Nola and Georgie laugh-smiled at each other.

"Isabelle is a weird eater," Nola said. "You'll get used to it."

"Yeah," said Georgie. "She hardly eats a thing."

"I noticed," Paula said, in a kind of snotty way, which made me want to chuck an egg at her.

"But we love her anyway," Nola added, which made me want to hug her.

Paula and Georgie were both eating the school lunch—some kind of chicken and rice with gravy, and green beans. For dessert it was cut-up peaches from a can, floating in syrup.

Nola was eating the same exact lunch she eats every

day: two peanut butter sandwiches on pumpernickel bread and two chocolate milks. Nola could eat peanut butter and chocolate all day long and not gain an ounce. She has the skinniest, palest little body you ever saw. Whenever she gets cold—which is a lot—her skin turns blue and marbley all over.

My stomach rumbled as I looked at everyone's food. I could have eaten all three of their lunches and still have been hungry, but the truth is I can't stand eating in the cafeteria with everyone watching me. If people are going to look at me, I'd rather eat too little than too much.

I took a bite of carrot stick and sprinkled salt on my hard-boiled eggs. I thought about everything I would eat later, when no one was around.

Georgie started talking about soap operas, as usual. She is borderline obsessed with soap operas. I mean, she will not miss two of them, which she secretly tapes during the day so she can watch them at night when her crazy mother is asleep. Nola and I are casual watchers, meaning we know all the characters, but we will not go into cardiac arrest if we miss an episode.

Paula wasn't even pretending to follow our conversation. Her eyes kept wandering over to the center table. Ashley's table. You could tell Paula wished she was sitting there more than anything.

Lotsa luck, toots. Basically if you're not on the field hockey team, and you don't have long shiny hair and a toothpaste smile and perfectly broken-in size zero jeans, you can forget it.

At the center table Ashley Barnum was busy smiling and tossing her hair while talking to Heather Jellerette.

Eli Bronstein, the cutest guy in our grade, came up behind her, pretending to dump ginger ale on her head. Ashley squealed so loud, everyone in the room turned around. "No, Eli! Don't!" Finally Eli picked her up and tossed her over his shoulder, sack o' potatoes style, while she whacked him on the butt with a lunch tray. Everyone at the table started clapping and cheering. Eli lowered Ashley into a chair. She sat up smiling, with pink cheeks and flyaway hair. "Eli!"

"God," said Paula. "Could they be any louder?" She was trying to act annoyed, but you could tell she was thinking, *Okay, here's the plan: I'm going to grow out my bangs and buy some cooler jeans, and then maybe . . .*

Nola just smiled and took a sip of chocolate milk. "They are kinda loud. You'll get used to it though."

Nola doesn't care about things like who's sitting at which table. Neither does Georgie.

I guess that's the difference between us.

5

WHEN I GOT HOME FROM SCHOOL my mother was on the phone with my Aunt Weezy. They're twins, but you wouldn't know it from looking at them. Sure, they have the same curly black hair and blue eyes, but Weezy wears makeup and clothes from Ann Taylor. She goes to kickboxing and gets her nails done. My mother looks like she just rolled out of bed and put on the first thing she could find, usually sweatpants.

It didn't used to be that way. Mom used to dress cool, with nice black slacks and funky jewelry. Not any more though. These days she doesn't even care if she matches.

Right now, she is spread-eagle on the kitchen floor, a ratty old skirt bunched up around her waist, flashing her panties to the world. On the linoleum between her legs sits a saucepan of boiled potatoes ready to be mashed. She is holding one of the potatoes in the same hand that is holding the phone and is actually *nibbling* at it while she chats. Some dignity, please!

Mom and Aunt Weezy talk at least twice a day. I call that ridiculous. Mom calls it a twin thing. Umbilical cord, phone cord. I'm glad Weezy lives an hour away from us, or she'd probably be over here twice a day too.

"How's Nini?" Mom was saying, scratching her thigh with the potato masher. She looked up and saw me in the doorway, waved.

I waved back.

"Really?" Mom said. "Awww. . . . How did you find out? . . . Uh-huh. . . . She came to you first? . . ."

My mother covered the receiver with one hand and whispered to me that Nini got her period! Yesterday!

Whoop-dee-doo. I've had my period since I was eleven. It's supposed to be this big deal, like you're all of a sudden a woman the minute it happens. And now, if you wanted to, you could get pregnant. Oooooo. Trust me, when you get it, it's not all that magical. You don't feel more grown-up or anything. Just crampy. And fat.

Anyway, I don't know why my mother would get herself so worked up over Nini. I mean, who cares?

My cousin Janine Barrett may be my age, but she is my polar opposite in every way. First of all, she is four-foot-six—practically a dwarf. And she's a gymnast, which means she competes all over the country and weighs about seventy-five pounds, leotard included. She thinks anything over eighty pounds is fat.

"Is Nini home yet?" my mother said. "I want to talk to her. I want to say congratulations."

I grabbed a few grapes from the bunch on the kitchen table and ran upstairs before my mother could make me get on the phone with Nini and congratulate her.

The last time I saw Nini, which was Thanksgiving, she made a comment I will never, ever forget. We were up in my room getting ready for bed, and we were standing in front of the mirror brushing our hair. I remember because it was the first time I'd ever seen Nini wearing a bra. She still didn't look like she needed one, but there it was. It had a little yellow butterfly in the center.

We were standing around in our underwear like we'd done a million times before, since we were two years old. No big deal. And then, she said it. "Wow, Isabelle. You're getting *big*."

"What?" I said. I wasn't sure I'd heard her right.

Nini kept right on brushing her hair. "What size are you now, anyway?"

I crossed my arms over my chest. "I don't know. My mom buys my bras."

"Not your *boobs*, dummy. I mean, what *size* are you?"

I opened my mouth to say *none of your business*, but no words came out.

Nini put her brush down on the bureau and turned to face me. "What do you weigh now, Belly? Like one-*ten?*"

I grabbed the closest thing to me, which was Nini's sleeping bag, and wrapped it around my body. I bit my lip hard, so I wouldn't cry.

True story. See why I'm not planning on talking to her anytime soon?

Upstairs, I lay down on Mom's bed and listened in on the phone conversation. This is not as hard as you would think. All you have to do is pick up the receiver really carefully and try not to make any sudden movements. Also, you should cover the mouthpiece with your hand in case you feel the urge to sneeze.

"You're not getting any younger, Beth," I could hear Aunt Weezy saying. "I hate to break it to you, but the big four-five is just around the corner."

My mother said, "For you too."

"True," Weezy said. "But, well . . . have you thought about kicking up your heels a little? Getting your hair foiled, maybe? Something?"

My mother snorted.

"Well?" said Weezy.

My mother said, "No, I haven't thought about it." And then she turned things around. "Have you thought about getting *your* hair foiled?"

Aunt Weezy didn't answer.

"Well?"

"Honey," my aunt said quietly.

"What?" said my mom.

There was a pause.

"What, Louise? Just say it."

"Bethy," Weezy said, her voice soft. "Won't you even think about starting to date again?"

I could feel my stomach contract, squeezing in on itself.

"Beth?"

My mother wasn't saying a thing, but I wanted to scream into the phone *NO!!! She won't think about starting to date again!*

"I know this is hard for you to hear," Weezy continued. "I know it's painful. But, honey, there comes a time when you have to . . . you know . . . life does go on."

"Louise," Mom said. She took a breath. "I'm fine. We're all . . . fine. Life is going on, in its way."

"Okay," said Weezy.

"Can you understand?"

"Yes. But this conversation is always . . . I mean, nothing is really . . . well . . . Bethy, it's been two years."

I wanted to scream into the phone, *One year and eight months, you idiot!*

When my mother spoke, her voice sounded like gravel. "What is it that you want me to do, exactly?"

"I don't know," said my aunt. "I don't know, honey. I'm sorry. I just . . . I hate seeing you so . . ."

"I'm fine. Really. We're all fine." In case you haven't noticed, *fine* is my mother's favorite word. *I'm fine, we're fine, everything's fine.*

"I know," Weezy said. "I know that."

"Okay?"

My aunt sighed. "Okay," she said. But you could tell she didn't mean it. She just had enough sense not to keep going.

I waited awhile before going downstairs. When I got there Mom was still lying on the kitchen floor, eyes closed, skirt bunched up. She and the potatoes hadn't moved in an hour.

I stood in the doorway watching her. I tried to imagine my mother on a date, sitting in a dark movie theater somewhere, wearing one of Aunt Weezy's Ann Taylor outfits. A purple sweater set maybe, with pearls. Next to her, some older guy in a blazer, gray hair gelled back into a helmet, one arm circling her shoulders. Next to him, on the other side, was me. Punching him in the face.

I cleared my throat, loud. "What's for dinner?"

Mom opened her eyes, which were red. "Oh, honey. Hi. I didn't see you there." She got up to walk the potato pan over to the counter. Her skirt was tucked into her underwear, and it looked so ridiculous I wanted to scream.

"If you think I'm eating your crotch potatoes," I said, "you're crazy."

Mom turned around. "Excuse me?"

"If you're going to make mashed potatoes sitting on the kitchen floor with the pan between your legs, I'm not going to eat them. Crotch potatoes."

"Cute, Isabelle," my mother said. "Very cute. Anyway, I'm making us a healthy meal. There's baked chicken. Skinless. Salad. Corn on the cob."

"I can't have corn on the cob," I said.

"Why not?"

"Hello?" I pointed to my mouth. "Braces?" Sometimes I wonder if my mother knows anything about me.

"Right," she said. "Well, you can cut it off the cob if you want, with a knife. It's easy."

"Whatever."

"I also got fresh strawberries for dessert. Okay? Everything healthy."

"Whatever."

"Isabelle. Enough with the *whatevers*, okay?"

"Fine," I said, picking up a few more grapes and walking toward the stairs. "And anyway, all I want for dinner is a salad."

Even though I knew that later, after Mom was in bed pretending to be asleep, I would get up and sneak downstairs and open the refrigerator door. I would take out the bowl of leftover mashed potatoes and eat every last bit of them with my hands. Standing up. Cold hard lumps of potato greasy with butter, washed down with half a quart of milk straight out of the carton.

And in the morning, no one would say a word about it.

6

THE NEXT DAY WAS GROUP. As soon as we sat down Trish handed out pens, the really nice felt-tip kind, with our names taped on the side. Even Rachel couldn't complain.

Trish asked us to take out our blank books.

"Journaling is a great exercise," she said. "It's a way to release some of that emotion building up inside you. You know how if you fill a balloon up with too much air . . ." Trish held both hands out in front of her and moved them farther and farther apart, making a whooshing sound out of the side of her mouth. Then, she clapped so loud we all jumped. *Pop!*

"Well," Trish continued, "emotions work the same way. If you don't find a way to let those emotions out, whatever they are—anger, fear, sadness—you can start to feel like you're going to explode. Writing is a way to let some of the air out of your balloon, before you pop, so to speak."

If Mr. Minx were there, he would be nodding up and down like crazy at Trish and her feeling-balloon. A+ *for use of figurative language*.

I was sitting on the same couch as last time, Mathilde on my right. I was glad that Dawn sat on my left, instead of Lila. Ashley came in late. Her cheeks were pink, like she'd been running.

"Sorry," she said.

Trish smiled. "Good to see you, Ashley. We're talking about journaling." She handed Ashley a pen.

"Thank you," Ashley said. She sat in Dawn's old chair and bent over to unzip her backpack.

Turns out, Ashley's journal is just a plain black memo book like mine. Funny, I expected something leather, with her initials engraved in gold or something.

Dawn's journal is covered in sunflowers. Mathilde's has a picture of a kitten on the front, dangling by its claws from a tree branch, with bright pink script saying *Hang in there*.

Our first journal assignment was to form two lists: on the left-hand page, the things we like about our bodies; on the right, the things we'd change if we could. We might be doubtful at first, Trish said, but once we gave journaling a chance, we would be amazed at what we could discover about ourselves.

"Um, Trish?" Lila raised her hand. "Does penmanship count?"

Please.

Trish said no, and neither did spelling. Journaling is just for us. Unless we want to share, the contents of all journals will be kept confidential. Ten minutes of journaling, starting now. Hmmm.

Things I like about my body: my feet

Things I'd change:
   my hair (brown: barf)
   my eyes (same)
   my ears (stick out)
   my nose (stubby)
   my braces (gross!!!)
   my fat arms
   my fat stomach
   my fat hips
   my fat butt
   my fat legs!!!

If Trish thought I was going to share this list out loud, she was crazy. It's not like anyone needed me to announce how gross I am. They could tell just by looking.

When I was done writing I started doodling all over the front of my journal. I'm pretty good at drawing vines. Also, tiny footprints.

According to the clock on the wall there were still six minutes left. If I were Ashley Barnum, would six minutes be enough for me to finish writing down every single thing I love about myself?

Lila was writing furiously in a notebook the size of her hand. Microscopic mouse-print, invisible to the human eye.

Mathilde's cursive, large and loopy like a little kid's, was easy to read. There wasn't one thing she liked about herself.

"Time!" said Trish.

She told us to close our journals and our eyes. "Now, raise your hand if you wrote down more things you *don't* like about your body than you wrote things you *do* like."

Obviously, this was some kind of test. Trish was checking to see if we're normal or messed up, right? Fine.

I raised my hand.

Trish told us to open our eyes but keep our hands in the air. "Look around," she said. "Everyone in this room has her hand in the air. So, if you think you're alone in this, think again. We're all in it together."

Rachel snorted.

I didn't blame her. Trish was grating on my nerves too.

But then, she surprised us. She told us to trash what we'd written. "Rip those pages out. Tear them into tiny pieces and dump 'em!"

Trish held the trash can up in the air, like it was a trophy.

"But, Trish," said Lila. She sounded like she was about to cry. "My pages aren't perforated."

"That's okay, Lila," said Trish. "Just do the best you can."

There was all sorts of ripping and tearing and crumpling of paper. We got to shoot baskets from wherever we were sitting.

Once all the paper was in the trash, Trish started telling us how the first battle we were going to have to learn to fight was our voice of negativity.

Huh?

Trish explained. "That little voice inside you that tells you you're too fat, or your thighs are too big, or you shouldn't eat this and you shouldn't eat that, otherwise you're a horrible person? That voice."

But what if you really are fat and you are gross and your thighs are too big?

"The trick," Trish said, "is to replace the voice of negativity with something that makes you feel good rather than bad. Instead of beating yourself up all the time, you can build yourself up by changing the dialogue in your head."

Rachel snorted again. I got the feeling she was going to be doing a lot of snorting.

Trish ignored Rachel and asked us to partner up.

Flashback: fourth-grade gym, picking teams for dodgeball. I was horrible at dodgeball. I was always one of the last kids standing, staring at my feet, while the captains argued with each other. "*You* take her. . . . No, *you* take her."

Trish had to have noticed that we were all staring at our feet because she said, "Okay then! Partners are . . .

Dawn and Mathilde . . . Lila and Rachel . . . Isabelle and Ashley."

Isabelle and Ashley.

"Don't move yet," Trish said. "Let me tell you what you're going to do. You're going to face each other like you're looking into a mirror."

Great. Me, playing Ashley Barnum's reflection.

"And you're going to take turns. First, one of you will say out loud something that your voice of negativity often says to you, like 'You look fat,' or 'You shouldn't eat that.' Something along those lines. Then, the other one of you will replace that voice with something positive, something encouraging. After a minute or so, I'll let you know it's time to switch. Okay? . . . Go to it!"

There was a whole lot of shuffling around and dragging of chairs. Ashley and I met in the corner by the window.

She had her hair in braids. There were skinny blue ribbons woven all the way through each one. You can tell Ashley's a real blonde because there are so many colors of blonde, from light brown underneath to almost white around her face. She has the prettiest hair you've ever seen in your life.

"Hey, Isabelle," she said.

"Hey," I said, scooting my chair in close and focusing on her knees, which were perfectly tan. Everything about Ashley is perfectly tan.

She said, "You want to be the negative one or the encouraging one first?"

"I don't care," I said. "Whichever."

"Sure?"

"Yeah."

"'Kay. I'll be negative to start."

"'Kay."

Trish told us not to hold back. "Be honest with your-selves," she said. "That's the way this exercise will work."

Somehow I knew Ashley Barnum was going to throw a zinger. She always follows directions.

"You look fat today," she said.

"Thanks a lot," I said. I knew she wasn't really talking to me, Isabelle. I was just the mirror. Still, when somebody like Ashley Barnum looks you straight in the eyes and tells you you're fat, you can't help but react.

Ashley's cheeks got all red. "Not *you*," she said. "*Me*. I'm talking to *me*. *I* look fat."

"Kidding," I said. "I'm just a mirror, remember? And no, you do *not* look fat. Um, your eyes look good with that shirt. Matchy."

Ashley was wearing a light blue scoop neck with a strand of darker blue ribbon woven along the edges, the same color as the ribbon in her hair.

"Thanks," she said, picking at her chin.

I didn't know what she was picking at. Ashley Barnum has absolutely no zits.

"Okay," she said. "Ashley? . . . Don't eat that third cup-cake, you fat pig."

"Ashley," I said. "Have the third cupcake. If you really want it. There's nothing wrong with the third cupcake, just like there was nothing wrong with the first two. It's a delicious, frosted treat, not a cardinal sin."

"Isabelle!" Ashley started busting up.

I made her laugh. I made Ashley Barnum laugh.

"I don't even want the third cupcake anymore," she

said, laughing. You could see the metal bands of her retainer. "Where are you when I need you? When I'm about to eat my five hundredth?"

Where am I when she needs me? Where am *I* when Ashley Barnum needs me?

Trish told us to switch, so we did. Now I got to be the mean one and Ashley got to be sweet as pie.

"Isabelle," I said, focusing on Ashley's chin. "You are disgusting. Stop stuffing your fat face."

"Isabelle," said Ashley softly, leaning forward and putting her hand on top of my hand. "You do not have a fat face."

I felt my cheeks get hot. "I don't?"

"No. You have great eyebrows."

"I do?"

Ashley leaned back and squinted. "Uh-huh. Delicate. Like bird wings."

"I never thought about my eyebrows before."

"Well, you should. They're one of your best features."

"Yeah, well." I didn't know where to look, so I looked at my feet.

"Okay," Ashley said. "Do another one."

This time I made eye contact. Ashley's eyelashes are so long, they look like they could get tangled up in themselves. "Face facts, Isabelle," I said. "Your thighs are gross."

"Your thighs are not gross," Ashley said, not even looking at my thighs. "Besides, did you hear that story on the news last week? About that girl? She had to have both legs cut off after a boating accident. She swam right into the propeller. You know? We could be her."

"She really doesn't have any legs?" I said.

"True story."

"Gross."

"Yeah. And sad too."

"Yeah," I said. "We *are* lucky not to be legless."

"I know it," said Ashley.

We sat for a minute, looking down at our legs and trying to feel lucky.

It's hard to feel lucky when your thighs are as disgusting as mine are. I hate sitting down because they squoosh out a mile wide. If I had Ashley's legs it would be a different story. Ashley's legs are long, thin, and tan. They look like they came from some supermodel mail-order catalog. I could feel the little hairs on my knees rubbing up against her smoothest of all possible legs.

I promised myself I would start shaving. Immediately. Who cares if my mother thinks thirteen is too young? She's not the one who has to sit leg-to-leg with Ashley Barnum.

"Hey," Ashley said. At first I thought she was referring to my hairy legs, but then I saw what she was looking at.

Over by the door, Rachel's voice sounded high and wheezy. "What are you talking about? You're a total stick!"

Trish was squatting next to Lila, her arm around the back of Lila's chair. "Rachel. Take a breath."

Rachel stood and kicked a table, sent a stack of magazines flying. "I'm *breath*ing!" She picked her umbrella up off the floor and slung it over one shoulder like a hobo stick. "You're all a bunch of whack jobs anyway!"

Rachel tried to slam the door on her way out, but a piece of umbrella fabric got stuck in one of the hinges, and it took her a second to yank it out. Then she tucked the umbrella under one arm, like a machine gun, and turned to take aim at Trish. "You better not talk about me when I'm gone!"

Slam!

Trish just stood there against the wall, blowing air into her bangs, which were damp enough to stand up straight on their own. We helped her pick up the magazines and push the chairs back into a circle. Then Trish started to tell us about how Group is kind of like a family.

Sure, Trish. The kind of family you'd buy at the Salvation Army.

"Sometimes families fight," Trish said, arranging magazines into the shape of a half-moon. "Sometimes they hurt each other. Or disappoint each other. Or make each other furious. But, in the end . . ." Trish walked to the middle of the room. "If they choose to . . ." She interlaced her fingers, two at a time. "They can come back together. Stronger than ever."

Try having my family for a day, Trish. Try going to bed with a dad and waking up without one. Try having a mother who's sad all the time but pretends she's not. Then we'll talk.

Over on the couch, Mathilde was sniffling. Dawn unzipped her backpack and took out a packet of mini-tissues. "Here," she said. "They're the soft kind."

When Mathilde blew her nose she sounded like a tuba.

"Thank you, Dawn," said Trish. "That was a really nice gesture."

Across the room, Ashley gave a little wave to get my

attention. She formed her hands into two quacking duck mouths. I rolled my eyes in agreement.

We were so bonded.

Ashley got a ride home with The Brothers, but not before she slipped me a scrap of paper with her number on it. 562-3343. Five six two, three three four three. I had Ashley Barnum's phone number. Ashley Barnum wanted *me* to call *her*.

I was so happy right then, I decided to walk to the bus stop with Dawn and Mathilde. We were all going the same way, it seemed silly to walk separately.

Nobody said anything for the first three blocks. Mathilde was still blowing her nose. But when we got to the bench outside the post office, she dove into her backpack and came up with a fistful of candy bars. "You guys want some chocolate? I've got Snickers, Reeses, Clark Bar . . ."

Dawn said, "Sure. Thanks, Mathilde." She took the peanut butter cups.

I started to say something about not snacking between meals, but I stopped myself. I took a Snickers. What the hey. I had Ashley Barnum's phone number.

Mathilde ate her Clark Bar surprisingly slowly, in tiny bites, like a beaver. She unrolled the wrapper as she went.

Weird. I would have thought that because she's so fat, Mathilde would eat really fast. It turned out Dawn and I were the ones who swallowed our candy bars in two bites.

"Help yourselves," Mathilde said. "There's plenty."

Waiting for the bus, Dawn ate three more candy bars, and I ate four. Then, when the number seven finally pulled up, I'm not kidding, I grabbed another two for the road.

7

GEORGIE CALLED JUST AS I was finishing my homework. If you're ever on the phone with Georgie on a school night, remember this: you'd better get off at eight o'clock on the nose or her mother will have a conniption. Sometimes she gets on the other line and says things like *Georgine Clancy Miner, you're going to stunt your growth if you don't get ten hours of sleep. You'll lose brain cells.* Mostly she rings a bell like Georgie is a cow and needs to get back to pasture.

Nola called at 8:01, exactly. "Hey, Isabelle."

"Hey."

"Did you just get off with Georgie?"

"Uh-huh."

"Did her mom ring the bell?"

"Naturally."

"Did you do your math homework yet?"

"Uh-huh."

This is how our phone calls go, the same conversation every time. I let my mind wander and pretended I was talking to Ashley Barnum, who I was too much of a chicken to call in real life even if she did give me her number. *Hey, Ashley. It's me, Isabelle.* If it was Ashley on the phone, we'd have all sorts of interesting things to talk about. We'd never want to hang up. Not like with Nola, who practically puts a person to sleep.

"So," she was saying. "Picture day tomorrow. It feels like we just had picture day, doesn't it?"

"I don't know. I guess."

"I think I'll wear my blue button-down. What are you wearing, Isabelle?"

For some reason this irritated me no end. I was perfectly happy daydreaming that I was talking with Ashley, and now Nola had to go ahead and bring up picture day, the one day where nothing I wear, short of a pillowcase over my head, will make an ounce of difference. I always turn out the same way, demented.

If you stand in the den and look at my school photos from over the years, you can see for yourself. Let's start with fifth grade: stitches on my chin, covered by a Band-Aid. Sixth grade: left eye closed. Seventh grade, the best ever: a piece of pancake stuck in my braces. Need I say more?

The den used to be my favorite room in the house. I used to love looking at all the photos. I remember this one of Mom and Daddy on their wedding day, all shining eyes and white teeth. And the one of Daddy and me at a football game when I was three, me on his shoulders holding a baton. And the four of us out on the porch in summer, April on Mom's lap and me on Daddy's, all making monkey faces. Best of all, the photo of Daddy in high school, wearing his baseball uniform, so handsome you can't believe you're related.

The problem with the den now is that he's gone. There's not one frame with him in it, and that hurts. Besides that, I can't ask my mother what she did with the photos because if I do she'll have a total breakdown, and I will be left feeling even more terrible than I did to begin with, if that's possible.

The reason I hate picture day is it's fake. You can smile for the camera as if to say, Look! I'm so happy! But then you get them back and you don't look that way at all. You just look pathetic.

"I'm wearing a burlap sack," I told Nola. "Belted. With my rainbow belt."

"Oh, Isabelle," said Nola.

She thought I was kidding?

"How about your green sweater, Isabelle? You look really good in green. It goes with your eyes."

If Trish was there she'd give Nola a gold star for her voice of positivity. But Trish was not there. "My eyes aren't green, Nola," I said. "They're brown. The color of poop."

8

PICTURE DAY, coming downstairs for breakfast. First thing my mother did was give me the Mom Look. "Such a pretty girl."

I said, "You're my mother. It's your job to say that."

"Well it also happens to be true." She snuck in a little cheek stroke, which I usually can't stand. But you see, she got up early to make breakfast for us. Most of the time she doesn't get out of bed until after we've left for school. It's only toast and cereal (Daddy would have made pancakes) but still. I didn't know whether to hug her or cry.

"Looks good, Mom," I said.

She began to glide around like an ice skater, pouring juice into coffee mugs. "Cheerios or Grape-Nuts?"

"Juice is fine. I have to get to school early."

Juice is not fine. She poured a whole bunch of Grape-Nuts into a bowl for me. "You'll have some cereal, then you'll go."

My mother has this habit of sounding Jewish even though she's not. *You'll have a matzo ball, some gefilte fish, then you'll go.*

The reason I know about sounding Jewish is I used to go to a Jewish day camp every summer. Beth El Temple Center Day Camp. All the moms who worked there talked in this particular way. They used a lot of Yiddish, calling me their little *maideleh*, which means sweet girl, or their little *holishkes*, which means stuffed cabbage. They were always pinching my cheeks.

Sometimes I think she talks Jewish to bring Daddy back a little, to not miss him quite so much. She would never admit it, not in a million years. I mean, we don't even celebrate Hanukkah anymore. But that's still what I think.

That's why I pretended to be excited about the Grape-Nuts, which, if you ask me, look like constipated mouse turds. "These are good, Mom," I said. "Is there fruit? For on top?"

My mother gave me a big smile and handed me a banana.

Ape Face showed up to breakfast in purple overalls— hand-me-downs from me, only I looked like a giant grape in them and she looks cute. She knows it too.

Ape Face stood in the doorway and cleared her throat. When she had our attention she did a little supermodel spin for us. "Well?"

"The perfect picture day ensemble," said my mother.

"Belle?" said Ape Face, in her sweetest little sister voice. "You look really pretty."

What is it with the compliments in this house?

"Uh-huh," I said.

Ever since the Bathroom Incident, Ape Face has been trying to kiss up to me. Not only is she full of compliments, she is also full of peace offerings. The night before, I found a jumbo bag of peanut M&M's and a container of sparkle lip gloss outside my door. On purple paper with glitter glue she'd written:

I'm sorry I got you in trouble, Isabelle.
I really am.
Love, April.

P.S. I bought this with my own allowance.

The M&M's were a nice touch, but she's going to have to work a lot harder to undo what she did.

"So?" my mother said. "How are your Cheerios?"

"Spectacular!" said Ape Face. There was milk running down her chin.

Mom reached over and smoothed her hair. "Thank you, sweetheart."

I choked down one last bite of mouse turds, the least I could get away with, and a few swallows of juice. "May I be excused? Please?"

My mother looked at my bowl. "You don't like the cereal?" she said. "You want something else?"

Yeah, I thought. *Pancakes.* "I'm not that hungry," I said.

Mom sighed. "Clear your plate, please, Isabelle."

Then, as I was heading out the door to meet my doom, "Belle? Sweetie? Don't forget to smile!"

The girls' room, ten minutes before first bell: hair spray so thick you could taste it.

Everyone was there.

"How do I look?"

"Is this lip gloss too shiny?"

"Can you see my bra through this shirt?"

Ashley Barnum's fan club was hogging the mirror, as usual. No one else could get a primp in edgewise.

Not that I came here to primp. No. I came to use the stall as it was intended, to spy. This is what you can hear if you hang out long enough in a girls' room stall:

"Does my pad show in these pants, you guys? Be honest."

"I can't tell. Bend over."

"I'm not bending over."

"Well, walk then, Danielle. Let us see you from behind."

"Okay. . . . So, seriously you guys. Can you tell?"

"Ally, where'd you get those jeans?"

"Gap."

"They're so cute."

"Did you hear Rose Gowan went to second with Jason Perry?"

"That lucky!"

"Euww!"

"I would never let Jason Perry go to second. I wouldn't even let him get to *first!*"

I had been at my perch for half an hour. I'm not kidding when I say I was perching, just like a bird on a branch. My feet were starting to fall asleep.

I was waiting for everyone to leave so I could check my teeth. I didn't need a repeat performance of last year's breakfast braces.

Through a crack between stalls I could see Heather Jellerette and her size zero jeans. I'd know Heather Jellerette just about anywhere. She is the second-prettiest girl in our grade next to Ashley. Plus, she's always wearing Guess? because her older sister works at the Guess? store in the mall.

As far as I could tell, she was the only one left. Heather was blotting her lip gloss with a paper towel. Blotting . . . blotting . . . blotting . . . leaving.

Was it safe to come out? Yes, it was safe.

Finally I could unfold myself, get some blood flow back to my legs. Except then I heard a sound coming from several stalls down, a sound that could only be one thing. Someone's breakfast coming up the same way it went down.

You had to feel bad for the girl who thought no one could hear her.

The toilet flushed, and out we walked together. Me and Ashley Barnum. Ashley Barnum and me.

Ashley wiped her mouth on the back of her hand. Her eyes were all red and watery. She saw me and just about died.

I didn't know what to say, so I just walked over to the sink and started washing my hands.

Ashley did the same.

There were no paper towels left, so we wiped our hands on our jeans.

When we came out of our state of shock, Ashley asked if I had any mints and I said, "Is Juicy Fruit okay?"

9

SOMETIMES THINGS HAPPEN in life that make no logical sense. Ape Face being nice. My mother getting out of bed before ten. And now, Ashley Barnum inviting me over to her house after school. I had no choice but to pretend it was really happening.

In a kitchen the size of Yankee Stadium, Ashley asked if I wanted to call my mom. "It's Friday," she said. "You can sleep over."

I found myself saying "Sure," as though I got invited to sleepovers all the time. The truth was, the only ones I ever went to were at Nola's, and those weren't all that exciting. Nola always falls asleep at nine o'clock, and Georgie ends up calling her mom to pick her up in the middle of the night because she can't fall asleep at all.

Ashley led me into a room with a lot of puffy green couches and leather chairs. Everything smelled like shoe polish and lemons. "Use this phone," she said, handing me a white cordless.

Ashley walked back into the kitchen so I could have some privacy. Good thing, too. You never know which of my mothers is going to answer the phone. Tired Mom, who can barely carry on a conversation and you know you woke her up even though it's the middle of the day. Sad Mom, who tries to act like she hasn't just been crying for five hours straight and when you ask if she's okay she says she's just coming down with a little cold.

This time I got lucky: Excited Mom. I had to take the phone away from my ear so I wouldn't go deaf. "That's wonderful, sweetie! A slumber party!"

"Mom," I said. "It's not a party. It's just me and Ashley."

She wanted to know what Ashley's like.

Nice, I told her. Pretty and nice.

"What about her parents? Have you met them?"

"Not yet. But I'm sure they're nice too."

"And they'll be around all night?"

"Mom, come on."

"Isabelle . . ."

"I'm sure they'll be around all night. Either that, or Ashley's brothers."

"How old arc hcr brothers?"

"High-school age. Old enough to drive."

"I don't want you getting in a car with Ashley's brothers."

"*Mom.*"

"Isabelle."

"Okay. I won't."

After I gave her Ashley's address and phone number, she asked if I needed anything. Pj's? Toothbrush? Sleeping bag? Underwear? "Just give me the word, Isabelle," my mother said. "I can be right over."

"I don't know," I told her. "I have to check."

Ashley called back from the kitchen that I didn't need anything, she had extra sweats and stuff.

"I'm all set, Mom. She's got extra."

My mother asked did we want her to swing by with something from General Cho's? Something healthy? Steamed chicken and vegetables? It would be absolutely no problem.

"No!" I said. "Definitely *not.*"

The silence on the other end of the phone said it all. I am a horrible daughter.

"Thanks, though, Mom, for the offer. . . . Um, next time?"

"Of course," she said. "Next time." But I could tell her feelings were still hurt. I am practically an expert at hurting my mother's feelings.

I made my voice soft and daughterly and told her I'd be home tomorrow morning, around eleven. "Maybe we could take a bike ride up to the lake?" I said. "Just the two of us?"

She liked this. "That would be great, sweetie. Have fun tonight."

"I will," I said. "Definitely." Then, "You have fun too, Mom. Okay? . . . Okay, Mom?"

"Okay," she said, but quiet, so you knew Sad Mom was back.

For dinner it was chicken marsala and some kind of fancy rice. I told Ashley's mother her cooking was delicious.

Mrs. Barnum dabbed at her mouth with a corner of napkin and said, "Thank you, darling, but I'm afraid I can't take credit."

Turns out they have a cook, Gregory. And he's *divine*. If I haven't tasted Gregory's spinach quiche, Ashley's mother told me, I haven't lived.

I happen to hate quiche more than anything, but I decided to keep this information to myself.

I was careful to cut everything into small bites and to finish chewing before opening my mouth. The only words I used were *please*, *thank you*, and *ma'am*.

Ashley barely touched her food, maybe one stalk of asparagus and that's it. The reason I noticed is that the portions were tiny. When someone wasn't eating, it was obvious. At least at my house, where everything is plopped onto your plate in one huge mound, you can always rearrange things to make it look like you're eating.

Even Ashley's dad ate only about two bites before he pushed his plate away, like he had better things to do. Mr. Barnum is that Richard Gere kind of handsome, with white hair and warm, crinkly eyes. He was wearing a tuxedo. I would say that he is older than Mrs. Barnum by at least ten years. Either that, or she's had a lot of plastic surgery.

"Kaye," Ashley's dad said to Ashley's mom and tapped his big shiny watch.

When Ashley's mother stood up, you could smell her perfume, spicy and exotic. Her dress was covered with about a million little green sequins.

"Warren," she said to Ashley's dad. "Go get the car."

Mr. Barnum gave her a yes-ma'am salute and clicked his heels together. He walked around the table to Ashley, kissed her on top of the head. "Night, Ash."

When Ashley said "Night, Daddy," I had to swallow hard to get the prickle out of my eyes.

"Isabelle," Ashley's dad said, bowing like Prince Charming. "A pleasure."

"Thank you," I said.

Ashley's mom gave us both air kisses and reminded Ashley to wash her face, twice, but not with soap. With the facial wash from Bliss.

On her way out the door, Mrs. Barnum threw on some kind of floaty scarf with a leaf pattern. She told us not to wait up because these functions at the country club run late. They would be back maybe one, two in the morning.

Oh well. What my mother doesn't know can't hurt her.

Out on the porch, Ashley's mom checked her hair in a little gold mirror. When Mr. Barnum pulled his big black car in front of the house, she slipped the mirror into a sequiny purse that matched her dress. "Good night, darlings."

"Night, Mom," Ashley said. "Have fun."

"Bye, Mrs. Barnum," I said. "Nice meeting you."

From the car, Ashley's dad called for us to hold down the fort. Ashley's mom said, if we wanted dessert, there were diet ice pops in the freezer. No fat.

In the kitchen, Ashley told me she was sorry about her parents.

"Why?" I say. "I thought they were nice."

"Yeah," Ashley said, with a little half smile. "Except for wanting to kill each other, they're a real treat."

I knew I was probably not expected to respond, but I nodded sympathetically. "Parents."

We were sitting on high stools at the kitchen counter. Ashley was picking at a hangnail on her pinky. It was her turn to speak, but I took it upon myself to break the silence. "Diet ice pop, anyone?"

Ashley said she could do better than that. How hungry was I?

"I could eat," I said. You have no earthly idea how much I could eat.

Ashley told me to follow her. We walked down a long hallway, into a pantry straight out of *Gone with the Wind*, big enough to hold a hundred salted pig carcasses. She started taking things off shelves. Chips, cookies, ravioli, peaches, tuna, cocoa, cereal. We headed back to the kitchen with a full load.

"So," Ashley said, dumping stuff on the counter. "Do you like salty first, or sweet?"

I told her sweet.

"Me too!" she said. She stopped and thought. "Bowls. Salsa. Soda." She asked if I wanted regular Coke or Diet. I said Diet. Of course.

I was directed to various drawers and cupboards, where I expected to find the same mismatched plastic cups and bowls we use at my house. I forgot for a moment that everything in Ashley's world is matching, everything is just so. Even the napkins were cloth, with a blue and yellow windowpane pattern that went with the stool cushions.

I held up a bag of corn chips. "Should I open these?"

"Yeah," said Ashley. "We'll lay everything out first."

She pulled two frosty mugs out of the freezer. They were so cold my fingers stuck to the handles.

Ashley poured two Diet Cokes, squeezing a little wedge of lime into each. "My dad is big into g and t's," she said. "That's how come I'm using lime instead of lemon."

"G and t's?"

"Gin and tonics."

"Oh. Right."

"Ever had one?" she asked.

"Not exactly," I said, as if you can kind of have a gin and tonic.

"What about wine?" she said. "My parents are big into red wine with dinner. Especially merlot."

"Yeah," I say. "I like red wine." For Passover Seder, Daddy would always pour a little kosher red into my glass. He showed me how to dip my pinky in and dab it on my napkin, ten times, to represent the plagues. Then we'd raise glasses and clink. "Lechaim, Bella," he would say.

Lechaim, Daddy.

Ashley opened the fridge and checked out the shelves. "I forgot! We have roast beef! And gravy! Want to make diner sandwiches?"

I said okay, and we set up shop. Baking sheet, saucepans, carving knife, fat slices of white bread, the kind that's really bad for you but tastes really good.

We piled everything onto a gigantic serving platter and schlepped it downstairs to the den, the only room in the house where we're allowed to make a mess. Ashley said her brothers practically live down there.

No kidding. It's only wall-to-wall posters of supermodels in bikinis. There's Ping-Pong, foosball, darts, and pool. Plus, a big-screen TV and a refrigerator. It's teenage boy heaven.

I asked Ashley, where *were* the brothers tonight, by the way?

"Jon and Dave are down the street, at Eric Dean's," she said, taking a single corn chip and dipping it in salsa. "You know Eric?"

I shook my head no.

"He's like my fourth brother." Ashley popped the chip in her mouth, chewed once, and swallowed. "And Craig's . . . where *is* Craig? . . . In the Hamptons, I think. Some party."

In the Hamptons. Where the rich people go.

I picked up my Diet Coke and swirled the ice around with my finger. "You don't mind being here all alone?"

"I'm not alone," Ashley said. "I have you."

Ashley kicked off her shoes and reclined on the couch, her feet propped on the coffee table. I noticed that her socks were pure white on the bottom. They probably smelled like vanilla beans.

I sat down next to her but kept my sneakers on.

Ashley sipped her Diet Coke and asked if I had any sisters or brothers.

"One sister," I said. "Younger."

"Really? A sister?" Ashley took her feet off the coffee table and tucked them under herself. "I always wanted a sister. How old?"

"Ten."

"Ten. You're so lucky."

I practically choked on an ice cube "You wouldn't want April for a sister," I said. "Trust me. She's a pain in the you-know-what."

Ashley smiled. She really does have the world's most perfect teeth. "Come on, Isabelle, she can't be that bad."

"Oh, yes," I said. "She can."

We continued the small talk for a few minutes. I tried not to look at the food trays. I wanted a chocolate chip cookie so bad I was drooling.

Finally, Ashley said, so casual, "I guess we should eat those sandwiches, huh? Before they get cold?"

Yes, I suppose we'd better.

And the corn chips, and the cookies, and the peppermint patties, and the Cap'n Crunch, and the tuna salad, and the cold leftover spaghetti, and an entire bag of frozen cocktail meatballs dipped in BBQ sauce, and the rest of the Diet Coke.

10

FOR OUR BIKE RIDE my mother packed us a picnic, all healthy stuff. Peaches, zucchini bread, and lemon hummus sandwiches on seven grain. Also a box of raisins, which I wasn't crazy about.

Besides that, there was a bigger problem. If I came within three feet of anything resembling food, I would die.

We'd been riding for a couple of miles. Every few minutes my mother pointed to a tree and announced how splendid it was. "Look at that one, Belle! Isn't it splendid? It's like fire."

I'll tell you what's like fire—my intestines.

"Ooo! Look at that one! Have you ever seen such colors?"

Somehow I managed to say "Wow!" and "Nice one!" But really what I was trying to do was stay vertical.

By the time we pulled off the bike path onto the dirt road that winds around the lake, my stomach was cramping so badly I was doubled over the handlebars. I told my mother I had to find a bathroom. Now.

She said if I could wait another mile, there was a gas station off Route 9.

"Emergency," I told her. "Number two."

Mom stopped and leaned her bike against the nearest tree. "Just give me a minute, sweetie," she said and began loosening her helmet.

I didn't have a minute. I had ten seconds, tops.

Rummage, rummage, rummage through the knapsack. My mother was *sure* she'd packed those paper towels. She was *positive*. . . . She could *swear* it. . . .

Too late! I was staggering through the woods like a rabid bear, unzipping my jeans and yanking them down around my knees. I was squatting, before I even found a tree. I was making noises that no human being should make.

It was pure torture.

If Ashley Barnum thinks I'm ever trying Ex-Lax again, she is insane.

My mother tucked me into bed with cool hands. She put a tray on my bedside table, some kind of broth and a stack of crackers. She sat on the edge of my bed and pulled the covers up to my armpits. "Feel better?"

I held up my hand to make the so-so sign.

"Any idea why your tummy's so upset?"

I did my best move: the shoulder shrug.

"Isabelle. A little feedback, please."

Just then a wave of cramps hit me. I pulled my knees into my chest and moaned.

"Belle? Honey? Do you need to use the toilet again?"

I didn't answer, I just tore off the covers and sprinted down the hall to the bathroom. I made it just in time. I stayed on the toilet for a long, long while. That gave me time to think.

When I got back to my room, Mom was still there, sitting on the edge of my bed.

I tried to make my voice cheery. "Well, that explains it! I just got my period!"

My mother held back the covers so I could crawl into bed again.

I babbled on. "You know, Mom, your period can really upset your stomach. I learned all about it in Health."

She nodded and handed me a cup with a bendy straw in it. "Take small sips," she said.

I swallowed. Ginger ale.

"What did you eat last night at Ashley's?" my mother asked. "Remember our deal about cutting back on junk? I hope you didn't have a lot of junk, Isabelle."

"I didn't."

"Anything that might upset your stomach? Anything rich? Ice cream?"

"Mom," I said. "I didn't eat anything." Just thinking about everything we ate made me want to run to the bathroom all over again.

"I thought you were having dinner there."

"I mean I didn't eat any junk. It's just period cramps. Honest."

My mother leaned her head to one side and looked at me.

"Although . . ." I said, wrinkling my brow like I was thinking hard, "I did have this chicken marsala thing. And you know what they say about undercooked chicken. I could have a very slight case of food poisoning."

Mom reached out to palm my forehead. "You are a little warm," she said.

"I feel a little warm," I said.

Even though I knew for a fact that Gregory-the-Cook would never poorly handle his chicken, maybe if she thought it was food poisoning she would stop asking so many questions.

"I should call Dr. Atlas," Mom said, "just to be safe."

"Oh no," I told her. "That's okay. Really. I'm feeling better already. See? I'm sitting up."

"Well . . ."

I almost had her. I took the tiniest spoonful of broth and dipped my tongue in it. "This is really good, Mom. Did you make it from scratch?"

"All right, Isabelle," my mother sighed, leaning over to kiss my forehead. "I'm going to take your word on this one. But if you start to feel worse, even by a millimeter, I'm taking you in. Deal?"

"Deal."

Around five, someone knocked on my door. It was Ape Face. Even though I didn't say she could come in, she marched right over to the bed and handed me a piece of orange paper cut into the shape of a sun. The glitter glue was still wet.

Get well soon Isabelle.
Love,
the only sister you'll ever have,
April Louise Lee

I gave her a nod, which was more of a Get Lost than a Thank You. But was she going to take the hint and leave? Oh no. Not Ape Face.

"Food poisoning," she said, like she was impressed. "That's bad."

I shrugged.

"The runs?" she asked.

"Uh-huh."

Naturally, she kept on going. Ape Face proceeded to tell me about this one time she had the runs, when she ate approximately five thousand grapes at a class picnic. For extra drama, she clutched her stomach and made farting sounds out of the side of her mouth. "I'm serious, Belly. I was, like, *exploding* with grape juice. I was a regular grape juice factory."

"Listen, April," I said. "This is not exactly what I need to hear right now."

"Oh," she said. "Okay. Do you feel any better yet?"

"Not really," I said, which was the truth.

Then Ape Face plopped herself right down next to me. "Scooch over," she said.

"What do you think you're doing?"

"Sitting," said Ape Face.

"I can see that. Did you think I invited you, or . . . ?"

Ape Face didn't say anything. She picked up a piece of my blanket and rubbed it between her fingers.

"Well?" I said.

"Isabelle?" Ape Face said. Her voice sounded shy, not like her usual voice.

"What?"

"I know you're still mad at me and everything, and well, I don't blame you. I really shouldn't have told on you."

"No," I said. "You shouldn't have."

"I know." She didn't look directly at me, so I kind of got that she meant it.

"Okay then," I said, meaning, You can leave now.

She didn't go anywhere though. She kept on sitting on my bed, rubbing my blanket between her fingers. Finally she said, "Belly?"

"What, Ape Face?" I said.

"Don't call me that," she said. "I hate it."

"Well, don't call me Belly."

"Fine. . . . Isabelle?"

"*What*, April? Spit it out, will you?"

Ape Face wouldn't look at me. She looked at the wall and said, "I have to do this project. You know, for school? It's this family tree thing. We need to write about everybody. And we need to have photos. So . . ."

I knew what was coming. It made me want to jam a pillow over Ape Face's big mouth to keep her quiet.

"I need your help, Isabelle," April said. "With the Daddy part. I mean . . . what do I do?"

I closed my eyes. Maybe if I kept them closed long

enough, she would go away. We could pretend this conversation never happened.

Here's the weird thing, on the day of the funeral April cried and cried. My mother didn't cry at all, and neither did I, but April wouldn't stop bawling. So how come now she can just talk about him like it's nothing?

"Isabelle? . . . Hellooo?"

I opened my eyes and stared at the ceiling.

"I didn't know who else to ask," said Ape Face. "I thought maybe you'd have some photos of him."

I shifted my position on the bed, bringing my knees up to my chest. "You thought wrong."

"Oh," said Ape Face. "Okay."

I closed my eyes again, but I could feel her looking at me.

"Isabelle?" she said softly. "Do you think she threw them all out, the pictures?"

I shook my head. It was easier than answering.

"Where do you think they are?"

I looked at her then. "How should I know?" I knew I sounded mean, but I didn't care. "Ask her yourself."

"God, Isabelle," she said. "Bite my head off, why don't you."

I closed my eyes.

"I only wanted some help."

I pulled a pillow over my face. The cool pressure felt good.

Ape Face got off the bed. She walked over to the door and just stood there. I could hear her breathing. All I wanted her to do was leave.

"Isabelle?"

Silence.

"You're not the only one, you know," she said softly. "I miss him too."

 **11**

I TOLD NOLA AND GEORGINE about having to
spend the weekend in bed. "I haven't moved in twenty-
four hours," I said. "Except to run to the bathroom."

"Rough," said Georgie.

Nola said, "I'm sorry, Isabelle. I wish you could come
over and do homework with us."

"Yeah," I said.

It was Sunday afternoon, and we were all three talking on the phone—me from my bed, the two of them from
Nola's house. I could picture them exactly. Nola would

be sitting cross-legged on the green corduroy couch in her living room, twirling a piece of long brown hair with one hand and holding the phone with the other. Georgie would be lying belly down on the yellow rag rug in Nola's room, bushy eyebrows scrunched together tight, trying to talk and do her math homework at the same time.

"Hey, where were you Friday night?" Georgie asked. "I called, but nobody answered."

It's amazing how quickly a lie can pop out of your mouth when you need it to. "At the movies," I said. "With Mom and Ape Face."

"What'd you see?" Nola asked.

"Some stupid Disney thing. I slept through half of it."

It's not that I think they'd be mad at me if I told them I spent the night at Ashley's. They just wouldn't get it. They'd want to know how it happened. How did we know each other, Ashley and me. Then, I'd have to A) lie some more or B) tell them about Group. And I didn't want to do either.

It's weird. We used to be really close, Nola, Georgie, and me. Our parents called us the three amigas because we did everything together. We were always over at each other's houses, or going places with each other's families. After my dad died, though, it was different. Nobody knew how to act around me anymore, even my best friends. They said things like adults would say: *I'm sorry about your father, Isabelle*, and *Maybe if you got out of bed and got dressed, you'd feel better*. But what did they know? They still had their dads.

Going over to their houses was even worse. Their moms would hug me so hard I couldn't breathe, or they'd just look at me with tears in their eyes. *Isabelle, honey. It's so good to see you. How are you? How's your mom?* Every time they did that I would think about my dad. And every time I thought about my dad all I would want to do is eat everything in sight, which you can't exactly do at some-body else's house.

Pretty soon a person gets tired of saying *I'm fine. We're fine. No, thanks, I'm not really hungry.* So you stop going over to people's houses. Then, after a while, everyone stops asking how you are.

Later, the phone rang again.

My mother knocked on my door. "Isabelle? It's for you, honey. It's Ashley."

It's Ashley!

As soon as my mom was out of earshot I could talk. "Ohmygosh, Ashley," I said. "You won't believe what hap-pened when I got home from your house."

Before you knew it we were talking away on the phone. Isabelle Lee and Ashley Barnum, shooting the breeze. It was actually not as weird as you would think.

"Anyway, my stomach is still killing me," I said. "Is yours?"

"Listen, Isabelle," said Ashley. "You have to give your body time to adjust. To flush itself out. Plus, you really should alternate between throwing up and Ex-Lax, other-wise you could really mess up your system."

"How come you know so much?" I asked.

"I read a lot."

"Oh," I said. "Well, thanks for the advice."

"No problem," Ashley said.

I was still in bed with the covers pulled up to my ears. I was curled up in a ball because when you've got the runs, that's the only position that works. Every time I tried to move, my stomach roared like Mount Vesuvius getting ready to erupt. I was pretty sure I'd have to stay in bed for the rest of my life, whereas Ashley got up at six a.m., did two hours of aerobics in her basement, took a bath, and finished all her homework.

She might not be human.

"So," Ashley said. "Do you think you'll make it to school tomorrow?"

"I don't know yet. It depends how I feel in the morning."

"Well, I hope you feel better."

"Yeah," I said. "Me too."

"Hey," said Ashley. "If you make it to school, maybe you want to sit with me and my friends at lunch?"

Maybe? Is she kidding me?

"Sure," I said casually, like I get asked to sit at the center table every day. As soon as I said it though, I thought about Nola and Georgie. I pictured their faces when I went to sit with Ashley instead of them.

"Well, I gotta get going, Isabelle," Ashley said. "See you tomorrow?"

"'Kay," I said. "See you tomorrow."

I hung up the phone and pulled my knees in tight to my chest, giving myself a little hug. Nola and Georgie had each other. I had Ashley.

At around six o'clock I got out of bed and hobbled downstairs. In the kitchen, my mother and April were all cozied up together at the table, studying for April's social studies test. The whole room smelled like tomato soup.

I watched from the doorway.

"Okay, April," my mother was saying. "I want you to name the original New England colonies."

Ape Face was eating a grilled cheese cut into quarters. "Easy," she said, squeegeeing ketchup off her plate with one of the triangles. "Massachusetts. Rhode Island. Connecticut. New Hampshire."

"Wonderful!"

Normally I would get mad, seeing April suck up all Mom's attention. Tonight I was feeling pretty good, though. I was thinking about tomorrow, having lunch at Ashley's table.

"Hi," I said from the doorway.

"Isabelle!" Mom said. She came over and gave me a big hug. "Feeling better?"

"A little," I said. I walked over to the table and sat down. I took a grilled cheese off a platter and poured myself some milk.

April ignored me and began telling my mother how she was going to memorize the thirteen original colonies in the order they entered the Union.

"First, I picture a CorningWare dish, right? Corning-Ware, for Delaware. Get it? Inside that, I imagine a bunch of chopped-up pencils, for Pennsylvania."

She went on and on. A girl named Carol in a bikini for South Carolina. A ham for New Hampshire.

"Clever!" said my mother. "Isn't that clever, Isabelle?"

"Uh-huh," I said, swallowing a bite of grilled cheese. "That's pretty good, April."

Ape Face looked up at me, suspicious. You could tell she thought I was being sarcastic. When she saw I meant it though, she looked really happy. "Thanks, Isabelle."

"You're welcome," I said, and I even smiled at her a little. Because for the first time in a long time I was not thinking, *Everything stinks*. Well, maybe everything did still stink. But tomorrow could be an okay day.

 12

AT LUNCH THE NEXT DAY I chickened out. I took one look at Ashley and her friends and lost my nerve.

So I parked myself at one of the corner tables as usual, with Georgie, Nola, and Paula. I was in the middle of pulling my lunch out of its brown paper bag, a kid-size container of strawberry yogurt and two Fig Newtons, when I heard Ashley's voice. "Hey, Isabelle."

I looked up and there she was, wearing a lavender shirt with silver sparkles all over it, and her big white smile. "Want to come sit at our table?"

"Um," I said. I felt my cheeks gather into a smile so big

I had to duck my head to hide it. I didn't want to make Nola and Georgie feel bad. I said to them, "You guys don't mind, do you? Just for today?"

Nola looked at me and shook her head the tiniest bit. "Do what you want, Isabelle."

"It's a free country," Georgie muttered, looking down at her tray.

Paula said nothing. I knew the minute I walked away she would talk about me, but at that moment I didn't care. She was jealous and I was glad. Paula could say whatever she wanted.

I busied myself with the complex task of putting my yogurt and Fig Newtons back in their bag. When I said good-bye to Nola and Georgie I tried to act like it was no big deal, me leaving them, but deep down I knew that it was.

The center table. Me.

When we got there Ashley swept her hand through the air, introducing everyone, as if I didn't already know all their names. "Isabelle, this is Maya, Arielle, Jessie, Hannah, Heather, Talia, Sasha, and Eliza. Everyone, this is Isabelle."

A couple of girls said, "Hi, Isabelle." The rest just stared at me.

"Hi," I said, sounding like a five-year-old.

Ashley pointed to an empty chair, so I sat down. Heather on one side, Talia on the other. In the middle of the table was a family-size bag of potato chips, one of pretzels, and a pile of Ding Dongs and Twinkies and individual Twizzlers wrapped in cellophane.

"Have whatever, Isabelle," Ashley said, motioning to the pile. "We take turns bringing snacks."

I sat quietly, eating my yogurt, one tiny lick at a time. I

wanted so bad to reach out for a Twinkie, and a handful of chips, but I didn't let myself. I knew that once I started I wouldn't be able to stop, and everyone would see me stuffing my face like a pig.

I noticed that Ashley wasn't eating much either. Every few seconds she took a bite of the green apple on the table in front of her, but that was it.

Everyone else dove right on in. There were hands everywhere—hands in bags, hands ripping open cellophane, hands in mouths.

At one point, Ashley got up from the table to get a drink from the water fountain. Talia turned to me. Her long red hair, smoothed back in a green ribbon headband, brushed against my wrist. "Promise you won't get mad if I ask you a question?"

"Okay," I said.

"Are you new this year? I've never noticed you before."

I could feel everyone's eyes on me as I mumbled, "I've lived here my whole life."

"Oh," Talia said. "Sorry." She didn't sound one bit sorry.

I kept on eating my yogurt, not saying anything while everyone else talked. Ashley came back to the table and sat down.

"Get a load of Big Bri," Heather Jellerette said, gesturing with a potato chip across the cafeteria. "Check out the high-waters. Did he raid his father's closet or what? What a dork."

We all turned to look. Over by the garbage can, unwrapping an ice-cream sandwich, was Brian King. His plaid pants were a little short, and tight too. His stomach rolled over the top of his belt.

"What a dweeb," said Talia.

"Dare me to go over there?" Heather said. "Tell him I like his pants?"

Everyone at the table started laughing.

I looked over at Ashley. She didn't look like she thought it was very funny, but she was laughing anyway, a fake laugh. *Heeheeheeheehee*.

"Come on, Heather," Talia said. "I dare you."

"Go, girl," said Maya, taking a dollar bill out of her pocket and laying it on the table. "Ice cream's on me if you walk over there and say, 'Hey, Brian, I've been watching you across the caf, and I just wanted to tell you, you look really, really good in those pants.'"

Heather stood up, tossing her hair over her shoulder and giggling. "Okay, you guys."

Everyone laughed and elbowed each other in the ribs. I just watched. I couldn't believe they thought this was funny. I couldn't believe even more that Ashley wasn't doing anything about it. She's always so nice to Brian in class, but when it comes to being nice to him in front of her friends, she doesn't have the guts.

Within five seconds, Heather was by Brian's side at the garbage can; her hand was on the back of his neck, and she was smiling. Heather leaned over and whispered something in his ear. Brian's face said that he believed her. He looked like a jack-o'-lantern, all lit up from inside.

"Oh, man," Heather said when she came back to the table, out of breath. "He totally bought it, you guys!" She stopped and looked around at everyone, eyes resting on me—the only one at the table not laughing. I can't make myself laugh when I don't think something's funny.

I looked at Ashley, watched her fake laugh some more. When Ashley saw me looking she looked away from my eyes, then down at the table, then up again at the rest of them.

"Man," Heather said, slapping her hand against the table. "He said, 'Th-th-thank you, Heather. I, I, I l-like your pants too.' What a riot!"

Heather grabbed the dollar bill lying on the top of the table and held it up in the air. "Free ice cream for me."

Ashley looked at me again, then quickly looked away.

I looked at her and thought, *Nice friends*.

When I got home from school the house was quiet. Ape Face was at ballet, which she has every Monday and Wednesday. Most of the time my mother is sitting at the kitchen table grading papers, waiting for me. Other times she is in bed, at three thirty in the afternoon.

I found out by going upstairs and standing outside her bedroom. "Mom?" I whispered. Then, louder, "Mom?"

She didn't say anything, so I cracked the door open. The shades were drawn and she had the covers pulled up over her head. "Mom," I said. "What are you doing?"

She stayed there in a lump, silent. At first I was scared, but then I saw the covers moving up and down so I knew she was breathing.

I took a step closer to the bed. "Mom. Are you sick?"

When she spoke she sounded far away, like she was at

the bottom of a well. "I'm fine, Isabelle. Just a little tired, that's all."

I wanted to pull the covers off her. I wanted to say, Why are you so tired? Huh? But I knew she wouldn't tell me the truth. Not in a million years would she say it: she can't sleep at night because she can't stop missing him.

I thought about what April said yesterday, when I was the one in bed. *You're not the only one, you know. I miss him too.*

"What about April?" I said. "Don't you have to pick her up?"

"Hmmm?"

"Mom!" I spoke like she was ninety years old. *"Don't . . . you . . . have . . . to . . . pick . . . April . . . up . . . from . . . ballet?"*

From underneath the covers she mumbled, "Carpool. Sara Winston's mom is . . ." Her voice trailed off like she was too tired to finish the sentence.

"Oh?" I said loudly, as if my old deaf mother was still participating in the conversation. *"Sara . . . Winston's . . . mom . . . will . . . be . . . picking . . . her . . . up? Okay! Great!"*

I felt so angry I wanted to shake her.

Instead, I took $20.00 out of her purse. I rode my bike into town. At Pay 'n' Save I bought $19.98 worth of Pringles, HoHos, and Diet Coke.

To the checkout lady, I said, "I'm having a study party tonight. Me and some of my friends from school."

I lined my items up on the conveyor belt. Five cans, four boxes, three bottles. "Thought we might need a little snack, you know? Brain power? There's gonna be four of us. Me, and my three friends."

The checkout lady, wearing green eye shadow and a lot of cheap-looking bracelets, looked at me like I had three heads. "Uh-huh. Paper or plastic?"

"Plastic, please."

Behind the Shoe Barn, I alternated handfuls of potato chips and HoHos with swallows of Diet Coke. The bubbles burned my nose and made my eyes water, but I didn't stop. It always feels better coming up than going down. You just have to get yourself to that point and then everything takes care of itself.

I slid my fingers inside my mouth and down my throat. I pushed and pushed until my knuckles reached the soft place in the back, the gaggy part. I held the plastic bag in both hands and watched everything come back up. Diet Coke, HoHos, chips.

Afterward I tied the handles together so nothing would leak out. In the garbage can out front, I buried the bag under a shoe box. *Chocolate Lorena, Size 6M.*

I got home about fifteen minutes before Ape Face did. When she came in the door I was in the kitchen making macaroni and cheese.

"You're cooking?" she said.

"Yeah." I poured more milk into the pot and stirred.

Ape Face plopped her tote bag on the floor and walked over to the stove. She was still wearing her pink leotard and tights. "Mac and cheese?"

"Yeah."

"Yum." She leaned in to take a whiff. Then she said, "Where's Mom?"

I gave the pot a couple more stirs before I answered. "Upstairs," I said. "In bed."

"In bed?" said Ape Face. Her voice sounded small. "What's wrong with her?"

"You know," I said. "She gets tired sometimes."

Ape Face hoisted herself up onto the counter and wrapped her arms around her knees. Her ballet slippers had black marks all over them. I wanted to tell her to get her dirty feet off the counter, but the look on her face stopped me. That, and how long her bangs were. She needed a haircut. Didn't my mother notice anything around here?

"Isabelle? She's not sick, is she?"

"Of course not," I said.

"How do you know?"

"I just do, that's all."

"But what if she is?"

"She's not! Okay? She's not sick. Trust me."

"Okay." April leaned over and rested her top teeth against her kneecap, biting down. She looked like she might start crying any second.

"Hey . . . ," I said. "Don't eat yourself. We've got a whole pot of mac and cheese here. Much tastier than your knee."

Ape Face lifted her head. She tried to smile a little.

"Come on," I said. I held out my hand to help her down from the counter. "We can watch TV while we eat."

13

ON WEDNESDAY TRISH handed out magazines. *Seventeen*, *YM*, *Self*, *Glamour*, *Elle*. She told us to take a few minutes to flip through them.

Ashley and I sat next to each other on the couch, sharing a *Seventeen*. Rachel didn't show up, so everyone was shifted.

"Look at this girl," Ashley said, pointing to the model on the cover. "She's perfect."

"I know," I said. "Her boobs are two perfect spheres."

"Double bubble," said Ashley, and we both cracked up.

We flipped to the survey. *Calculate Your Flirtability Quotient.* Not surprisingly, Ashley scored the highest possible mark, an 18. She is *The Life of the Party.* With a whopping 6.5, I am *The Wet Blanket.*

A few minutes later, Trish asked us to stop reading. She wanted to know what these magazines tell us out about ourselves. "Mathilde?" Trish said. "Would you like to start?"

Mathilde ducked her head. She was wearing barrettes in her hair. Green plastic turtles.

Holding her magazine up in front of her face, Mathilde whispered, "This is what I'm supposed to look like." With one finger, she tapped a picture of a blonde in a flowered bra.

Trish nodded. "Thank you, Mathilde."

Mathilde lowered the magazine and let her hair fall in front of her face.

"Dawn?" Trish said. "What do you think?"

Dawn shifted a few times in her seat. "Um . . . if I want to lose ten pounds by Christmas? I should try this new soup diet." She held up a picture of a model doing stomach crunches with a bowl of soup resting on her abs.

"Good," said Trish. "Good. . . . What else? Lila? Any thoughts?"

Lila was sitting alone in the corner, with her sweater pulled over her knees. As usual, her fingertips were tap, tap, tapping against her kneecaps. She didn't respond to Trish's question, she just stared at the carpet.

"Okay, Lila," Trish said, walking over to touch her on the shoulder. "Okay . . ."

"Trish?" Ashley was speaking, and I was surprised. She hardly ever says anything in Group.

Trish turned around and smiled. "Yes, Ashley?"

Ashley used her hands to help her talk, just like she does in English class. "Well, these girls, in these magazines. They all look so perfect, right? But maybe underneath all that . . . *perfect* . . . it's not so great for them. Like what if they got a bad grade, or they got in a fight with their friends? Or their parents are getting a divorce, or something. You know? You can't always tell, just from looking."

Trish nodded. "Good, Ashley."

It's amazing how Ashley knows just what to say in every situation. Where does she come up with this stuff? I know what she'd say if I asked her. *I read a lot, Isabelle.*

"Okay," Trish said, looking around at us. "Let's think about this. What about this idea that we have two sides — one that we show to the outside world, and one that we keep in, maybe even hide? Are there things people wouldn't necessarily know about you, just from looking?"

I pretended to be busy biting off a hangnail, but I was really thinking, *Yeah. Lots of things.*

Nobody said anything.

Trish put her fingers together in a steeple. "I know," she said. "This can be hard stuff to talk about. Why don't we get out our journals?"

Except for the first two pages, my journal is completely blank. Trish wants us to write in them at home, whenever we feel what she calls HALT feelings, which means hungry, angry, lonely, or tired. A couple of times I tried to make myself sit down and write, but nothing happened. I just ended up chewing on my pencil and staring at the empty page.

It was like when I used to try to talk to my mom after Daddy died. I would start telling her how sad I was, how much I missed him, but right away she would cut me off. "No, Isabelle. We're not going to do this. I can't do this." Pretty soon I knew not to bring him up. I made my mind blank instead.

The same thing was happening now. Lila, Dawn, Mathilde, and Ashley were write, write, writing away. What was I doing? Blanking out. Drawing miniature vines and tiny footprints.

As I doodled though, Trish's question started bouncing around my brain like a pinball. *What wouldn't people know about me, just from looking? What wouldn't people know about me, just from looking?*

Pretty soon the answer started bouncing around too. *They wouldn't know my dad is dead. They wouldn't know how much I miss him.*

Sometimes thinking something is just as hard as writing it.

When Group was over Trish stopped me on my way out the door. "Isabelle?" she said. "Got a minute?"

I paused in the doorway, backpack half on. One step ahead of me, Ashley paused too. She turned, caught my eye, raised one eyebrow. I shrugged back.

"Uh, Trish?" I said. "I've got to catch a bus, so . . ."

Trish smiled. "This won't take long."

Why do I feel like I'm in trouble? Am I in trouble? Trish is going to yell at me for doodling when I should have been writing.

I looked at Ashley. She was already walking backward down the hall, holding her hand to her ear like it was a phone.

I nodded and watched her backpedal down the hall, around the corner to the elevator. I thought about running after her, making a break for it.

"Isabelle." Trish touched my arm. "You're not in trouble."

"I know," I said.

"Would you like to sit?"

"That's okay," I said. "I like standing." I shifted my backpack so it was all the way on. I kept one hand on the doorknob.

Trish hoisted herself up onto the back of the couch and let her feet dangle. I noticed she was wearing the same kind of sneakers my mother wears, plain white with blue bottoms. "How are you finding Group, Isabelle?"

"It's okay," I said, focusing on a stain in the middle of the orange carpet. The more I squinted at it, the more the stain looked like a yawning dog.

"Good," Trish said. "What would you think about finding another time to meet with me? Just the two of us."

"What?" My head jerked up like a yo-yo. "Are you kicking me out?"

Trish shook her head slowly. "No. Our one-on-one time would be in addition to Group, not a substitute."

"Why?"

"Why a one-on-one?" Trish said. "Or why am I asking you, as opposed to someone else in the Group?"

"I don't know. Both, I guess."

"Those are good questions, Isabelle. First, I'd like to get to know you better. And second, everyone in Group will be working with me privately at some point. It's part of the process."

I shifted my gaze back to the yawning dog.

"I'm asking you now because I think there's a lot on your mind. And I think you may feel more comfortable sharing some of your thoughts and feelings when there aren't so many eyes on you. What do you think?"

It was hard to shrug my shoulders with a backpack on, but I tried.

Trish didn't say anything for a minute. Neither did I.

Then she said softly, "Is there someone else you'd rather talk to, Isabelle? Another adult? Someone you trust? A teacher maybe, or a relative. It doesn't have to be me."

I thought about Aunt Weezy. Last night on the phone she asked, "How are you sweetheart?" just like she always does. And I said, "Fine," just like I always do. What am I supposed to say when Weezy doesn't even know about Group? She and Mom talk twice a day, but Mom never tells her anything that matters.

"Isabelle?" Trish said. "Can you think of anyone you'd prefer to talk to?"

I shook my head no.

"How about meeting with me, then? Thursday at four?"

"I can't."

"Thursdays don't work for you? Do you have another commitment?"

I said the first thing that popped into my head. "I'm on student government." Even though I haven't been to a student government meeting since sixth grade. I used to do a lot of different things after school. Now I pretty much just go home.

"Student government," Trish repeated. "I didn't know that. That's great. How about Tuesdays then?"

I didn't say anything.

"Isabelle? Tuesdays at four? Does that work for you?"

I shifted my gaze from the yawning dog to the tips of Trish's sneakers. "I guess. I have to check with my mom."

"Do that," Trish said. "And then give me a call."

Trish reached into the breast pocket of her shirt and took out a little white card with some phone numbers on it. "You can call either number, any time."

I shoved the card in the back pocket of my jeans.

"We'll start next Tuesday, Isabelle," Trish said.

Next Tuesday. Yippee.

 14

ON SATURDAY MORNING Ashley and I went to Jessie's Place, this diner in her neighborhood. "I'm starving," Ashley said. "I could eat one of everything."

"I know," I said, even though my stomach was still churning. When I stay over at Ashley's all we do is eat. Last night her parents were gone again, so we ate half the kitchen.

"I hope they have chocolate chip pancakes today," Ashley said. "Sometimes they run out."

"I've never had chocolate chip pancakes," I said.

"Only blueberry."

"Chocolate chip are way better. Trust me. Sweet and salty at the same time."

The waitress, bleached blonde and skinny, stopped at our table. She handed us waters and menus and took our drink orders: two large hot chocolates and two large OJ's. Then she moved on to the next booth.

Ashley looked at her menu for about two seconds. "Want to get chocolate chip pancakes, scrambled eggs, and a Belgian waffle, and split?

"Yeah," I said. "And a corn muffin."

"Yeah."

It's funny. When we first started hanging out I didn't want Ashley to think I was a pig, so I was careful not to eat too much in front of her. I ate, just not as much as I would eat alone. Now, I don't even think about it. I eat whatever I want and so does she.

Ashley took a sip of water, settled back in the booth.

"So," she said, running one finger along the rim of her glass. "I'm going to Colorado over winter break."

"Really?" I said. "Colorado?"

"Yeah. Aspen. My family takes a ski trip to a different place every year. Last year it was Jackson Hole. I skied black diamonds with my dad and brothers the whole time and didn't wipe out once."

"Good for you," I said. I have never skied before, so I didn't know what else to say.

"Yeah," said Ashley.

"What about your mom?"

"Oh, she hates to ski," said Ashley. "She spends all day at the spa. Or shops in the ski shop for stuff we don't need.

She doesn't like to spend any more time with my dad than she has to."

"Yeah," I said. As if I knew exactly what she was talking about.

"What are you doing?"

"What? For winter break?"

Ashley nodded.

I took a swallow of water, put down my glass. "I don't know yet."

I did a little imaginative run-through in my head: me and Mom and April sitting around the kitchen table for two weeks straight, trying not to look at Daddy's chair. Everyone else is opening presents and hugging and playing in the snow, but there we are. Staring at a chair. Stuck.

We used to celebrate Christmas and Hanukkah. Christmas for Mom, Hanukkah for Daddy. The best of both holidays: tree, menorah, presents, candles, turkey, latkes. Now we just do Christmas. But not really. I mean, we don't jump up and down for joy or anything. Because, what's to celebrate?

I took another sip of water and looked up to see Ashley staring at me.

"What?" I said. I hate when people stare at me.

"Nothing. You just looked sad or something."

I thought about telling Ashley the truth. I imagined the look on her face when I said, *You'd be sad too if you didn't have a dad.* But I couldn't get the words out. "I'm not sad," I said. "I'm hungry."

"Yeah. Me too. Starved."

When the food came, it had a greasy sheen. You could tell by looking at it that the butter would melt onto your tongue and the syrup would slide like a sweet river down your throat.

Here we were, just two girls with lovely manners, sharing a meal.

"Could you please pass me a napkin?" I said.

"More salt?" asked Ashley. "Ketchup for your eggs?"

Before you knew it, we were both using our hands. Mopping, shoveling, stuffing. We must have finished everything in about sixty seconds. A record.

In back of the diner, we stood on crates and threw up next to each other into a dumpster.

When we were finished, Ashley wiped her mouth on the sleeve of her white turtleneck. "So. What do you want to do today?"

"I don't know," I said.

"We could go to the mall."

"True." I thought about what Nola and Georgie would be doing today. Going to the aquarium with their mothers, probably. For the millionth time. Or the stupid science museum.

I smiled at Ashley. "Let me go call my mom."

We walked down the block to the payphone. It was the kind with a door, so Ashley waited outside while I called.

"Lee residence," a woman's voice answered, surprising me.

"Aunt Weezy?"

"Isabelle? Is that you?"

"Yeah. What are you doing there?"

"Just a visit. I had to return some sofa cushions at Lowmans, so I thought I'd stop by and see my favorite girls."

She always calls us that: me, Mom, and April. Her favorite girls. I wonder what that makes Nini.

"How are you, sweetheart?" Aunt Weezy asked.

"Fine."

"Everything okay at school?"

"Yeah."

"At home?"

"Uh-huh."

Aunt Weezy lowered her voice. "And what about your mom? How do you think she's doing?"

For that one, I just let the little robot in me answer. "Fine," I said. "Everything's fine. So is she there, my mom?"

"In the shower, sweetie. I'm taking her out to lunch. And your sister. And you, if you're interested."

I told her no, that's why I was calling. I was on my way to the mall with my friend Ashley. Could she please ask my mother to pick me up in front of the movie theater, at say four?

"Is Ashley's mother going with you?" Aunt Weezy asked.

"Yeah," I said. As if she'd ever know the difference.

Weezy said all right. She'd tell my mom to pick me up at four.

"Thanks," I said.

"You're welcome," she said. "And, Isabelle?"

"Yeah?"

"Have a good time."

I hung up the phone and gave Ashley the thumbs-up sign. I was glad to get off the phone with Aunt Weezy. She asks too many questions.

Ashley walked the aisles of Lord & Taylor while I followed. We stopped at the one of the fragrance counters and tried on perfume. Ashley held up a bottle of something. "Hold out your wrist," she said, so I did. She gave me a big squirt. "Like it? It's Desire."

I took a whiff and tried not to gag. "Not bad."

"We'll take this," Ashley said to the lady behind the counter. "The biggest size you have, please."

The total came to eighty-six dollars. For perfume!

Ashley slid her father's credit card across the counter and smiled at me. "We'll wear this in Minx's class and drive him crazy."

Next we went to lingerie and tried on bras. Standing next to Ashley in the tiny dressing room, I finally didn't have any choice but to look at her up close.

Now I could see that she really is perfect. Her breasts are smaller than mine, but very round, and her stomach is flat as a board even after everything we ate. Her skin is light, light tan all over, the color of cream soda.

I tried not to stare at her, but I couldn't help sneaking little peeks. The sight of my own fat stomach and thighs in the mirror next to her made me want to cry. I kept trying to cover parts of myself up so Ashley wouldn't have to see all of me at once.

"That looks good on you," Ashley said, not even looking at the pink satin bra I had on. "You should definitely get it."

Ashley was wearing a matched set of white lace bra and bikini bottom, looking like a model. She was adjusting the straps and frowning at herself in the mirror, from every possible angle. Now she was pinching her thighs, hard enough to leave marks. "Gross," she said.

All I could do was shake my head. Did she really not know how pretty she was, or was she just trying to make me feel bad?

Finally Ashley said, "I don't care what I look like, I'm getting it. I'm getting it in every color they have."

After shopping, we went straight to Baskin-Robbins for sundaes.

"You know," Ashley said, her mouth full of whipped cream, "this is fun. We should do this more often."

"Yes," I said, not knowing whether she meant the shopping or the ice cream. "We really should."

In the woods behind the bus stop, we stood side by side, watching our sundaes come back up in reverse order. Ice cream first, then hot fudge, whipped cream, nuts, and finally, that red dot of cherry I swallowed whole.

When Ashley finished, she wiped her mouth on the back of her hand. It came back smeared with red.

"Ashley," I said. "I think you're bleeding."

"Am I?" said Ashley and spit into her palm. Blood. "Huh," she said.

"Are you okay?"

She looked at me and smiled. "Yeah! It doesn't hurt or anything."

"Okay," I said.

Ashley wiped her hand on her jeans. "It's no big deal, Isabelle. It just happens sometimes."

"Sure," I said. "No big deal."

 15

IT WASN'T MY MOTHER who picked me up, it was Aunt Weezy. I spent fifteen minutes looking for a red Toyota when I should have been looking for a green Volvo. I wasn't sure why she was there instead of Mom, but I wasn't about to ask. I just got in and buckled my seatbelt.

"It's good to see you, sweetie," Aunt Weezy said, leaning over to kiss my cheek.

"You too."

"Your mom's got a lot of grading to do, so I offered to pick you up."

"Okay."

Aunt Weezy looked pretty. Hair fluffed, lipstick, little drop earrings. This is what my mother could look like if she tried.

"Hey," Weezy said. "Are you hungry? I told your mom we'd pick something up for dinner. April wants pizza. How does that sound?"

I shrugged. "Okay, I guess."

"Pizza it is, then."

Aunt Weezy's car is like her, clean and neat. She listens to only one thing when she's driving and that's country music. She calls it food for the soul.

Weezy went to college in Montana. Her husband, my uncle Jack, is from there. Missoula, the town is called. He speaks with an accent. He also has a beard and wears Wrangler jeans. I like him, even if he is Nini's father. Nini doesn't deserve him.

When we pulled into the parking lot of Illiano's Aunt Weezy unbuckled her seatbelt, but she didn't get out of the car. She sat with her hands on the wheel for a minute. Then she turned in her seat to look at me.

"Isabelle." She paused. Out came the same question she asked on the phone earlier. "How do you think your mom's doing?"

I fiddled with a button on my coat. "What do you mean?" If Aunt Weezy said one word about my mom and dating I was getting out of the car. I didn't care if I had to walk home.

"I don't know," she said. "I can't figure out what's going on. She just doesn't seem like herself. She's . . . distracted."

I pulled on my seatbelt, stretched it out in front of me, and let it snap back in again. "Well, she's busy. You know. She has a lot of grading to do and everything."

Aunt Weezy frowned. "I don't know. Maybe she's working too hard."

"Maybe," I said, even though I knew Mom was only working part-time now, teaching only two courses. Aunt Weezy wasn't supposed to know.

"I don't know," she said again, shaking her head. "Maybe she should go and talk to someone. I tried to get her to go, after your dad died, but . . ."

That's what Weezy does. She just comes right out and says it. *After your dad died.* "She was just . . . in shock, I guess. She couldn't talk about him."

I pretended to be interested in my coat button again. There were lots of things in my head I wanted to say, but I couldn't. Everything was stuck in my throat like peanut butter.

"Oh, Isabelle. I'm sorry. I shouldn't have brought it up. I didn't mean to upset you."

"I'm not upset," I mumbled.

"I didn't mean to worry you."

"I'm not worried."

Aunt Weezy sighed. "Okay. . . . Anyway, I'm sorry. Let's just go get some pizza. Okay?"

We got out of the car and started walking across the parking lot. Right before we got to the door of the restaurant, Aunt Weezy put her arm around me and squeezed. "It's good to see you, sweetie."

I let my head rest on her shoulder for just a second before we went in.

On the way home I rode with the pizza on my lap, warming my legs. Whenever the box got too hot I'd lift it up, then put it back down. It smelled so good I could almost taste it. Nothing tastes as good as the first bite of pizza. Nothing.

Aunt Weezy was singing along with the radio, not exactly on key, but nice. I'll bet she sings all the time at home, in the shower, making dinner. I'll bet Uncle Jack does too. Maybe I should move in with them. Nini can move into my house.

I took some time to imagine the switch. Me, Aunt Weezy, and Uncle Jack sitting around the dinner table, singing, laughing.

In the real world, Weezy was pulling into the driveway right behind Mom's car. She was yanking up the parking brake and pulling her keys out of the ignition.

I took in a breath. "*I'm* going," I said. "To talk to someone, I mean."

Aunt Weezy turned, looked straight at me.

"On Tuesday. At four o'clock. I'm going to talk to someone. Trish, her name is."

Weezy put a hand on my hand and squeezed. "Oh, Isabelle." Then, "Does your mom know?"

I shook my head. It was too complicated to explain that Mom knew about Group but not about the one-on-one.

Still holding my hand Aunt Weezy said, very softly,

"You miss him a lot, your dad. It must be . . . well, you must miss him more than I can imagine."

I nodded. Stopped. Nodded again.

"Do you think . . . is this something you want to talk about with me?"

All I could do was shake my head. I knew if I opened my mouth I'd start crying, and maybe I'd never stop.

"Okay." Aunt Weezy said, squeezing my hand. "Okay."

On the porch, right before we went inside the house, Aunt Weezy hugged me hard. Me and the pizza. "It's going to be okay, Isabelle. It's going to be fine."

Fine, I thought. *It's going to be fine.*

Somehow the way she said it, I almost believed her. I wanted to. I really did.

 **16**

TUESDAY, FOUR O'CLOCK. Trish and I were sitting across from each other in her office, which smelled like Cheez-Its as usual. For some reason this made me mad. Didn't Trish ever think about other people's noses? Hadn't she ever heard of air freshener?

"Well, Isabelle, I'm glad you're here," Trish said. "I'm looking forward to getting to know you better."

"Yeah." As if I had any intention of spilling my guts.

"Are you comfortable?" Trish asked. "You can switch

chairs if you like." She gestured across the room. "Or move to the couch."

"I'm fine."

"Good. I want you to be comfortable."

I thought about this. Comfortable? "This isn't exactly how I want to spend my Tuesday afternoon, you know. With a shrink."

"A shrink?"

"That's what you are, right? A head shrinker? Someone who's supposed to shrink my problems?"

Trish smiled, leaned back in her chair. "That's one way of looking at it, Isabelle. . . . Okay, let's start there."

"Start where?"

"With any problems you'd like shrunk."

"I didn't say I had problems. I just said that's your job, to shrink them. If a person had any. Which I don't."

"You don't."

I shook my head and looked down at the orange carpet. There was that stain again, the one that looked like a yawning dog. If you squinted at it you could make it move.

"Isabelle," Trish said softly. "I'm going to ask you a question, and I'd like you to answer it honestly. Do you think you can you do that?"

I shrugged. "I guess."

"How many times did you throw up today?"

I thought about denying it. But I didn't. "Two."

"Do you see that as a problem, Isabelle? Your throwing up? Throwing up is natural sometimes. When a person has the flu or food poisoning, but making yourself throw up is a different thing. It's usually a sign that something else is wrong."

"Nothing's wrong," I muttered, more to the yawning dog than to Trish. But really I was thinking, *Yes it is.*

"Maybe *wrong* is a poor choice of words," Trish said. "Let me put it another way. Bingeing and purging—eating a lot of food and then making oneself throw up—can be a sign that something is bothering a person. Maybe she's sad. Angry. Lonely. Upset about something . . . and throwing up is a way of dealing with those feelings. Does that make sense to you, Isabelle? The way I've worded it?"

I shrugged, shifted in my seat, sighed.

After I'd shifted and sighed a few more times, Trish said, "It's your hour, Isabelle. I could sit here and talk the whole time but that's not really the idea. The idea is for you to be doing the talking, which I know is hard. Talking about feelings can be difficult, and sometimes scary, especially if you're not used to doing it. But let's say that this is a safe place for you to share those feelings. Okay? Let's say that this office is a place, and I am a person, you can trust. What do you say?"

"Okay. . . ." I took in a breath, looked up a little bit. "So. Let's say there is something bothering me."

"Is there?"

"There might be."

Trish nodded. "Okay."

"Am I supposed to just come out and say it?"

"That would be a good place to start."

I took another breath and looked at Trish. "I don't have a dad anymore. Okay? He died."

Trish leaned forward in her chair, looked straight at me. "How does it make you feel to say that?" She picked up the box of tissues on her desk and held it out to me.

I took one and held it in my lap. "I don't know."

"Having someone you love die is a horrible thing, Isabelle."

I nodded and bit my lip hard. I wasn't about to cry in front of Trish. "Okay, I have to ask you something."

Trish said, "You can ask me anything you'd like."

"Please don't say anything like 'If life gives you lemons, make lemonade,' or 'Just take it one day at a time.' I hate that."

"You mean like 'Every cloud has a silver lining,' and 'At least you have your health'?"

"Yes."

Trish said, "Do you think I would do that to you?"

"I don't know. But if you do, I'm leaving."

"Fair enough," Trish said. "I promise not to shower you with a bunch of clichés that don't help."

"Good."

Trish leaned back in her chair again and pressed her fingertips together into a steeple. "Okay," she said softly. "Do you think you can talk about your dad, Isabelle? Do you want to try?"

I nodded, a very small nod, but a nod. "I want to try," I said. And really, I meant it.

When I got home I called Ashley. "What are you doing?" I asked.

"Nothing. Homework. Where've you been? I tried to call you before but no one answered."

I lowered my voice just in case Ape Face was listening

in. "I was with Trish. Talking about . . . you know, stuff with me."

"Oh . . . huh."

"Yeah."

After a second Ashley said, "How come?"

"She practically made me. From last time? When she stopped me after Group to talk? She basically said I had to come and see her."

"Oh."

Ashley didn't say anything else, so I kept going. "We talked about . . . you know. *Stuff*. The same stuff we talk about in Group, I guess."

"Huh," she said again.

That's when I told her. I didn't plan to, the words just slipped out. "Mostly we talked about my dad."

"Your dad?"

"Yeah," I said. "My dad. He, well . . . died. Two summers ago. It was, like, a surprise. We didn't know he was sick."

When I finished telling her, Ashley whispered, "I don't know what to say."

"I know," I said. "No one does."

After I hung up the phone I went into my closet and sat on the floor, holding Daddy's shirt in my lap. I thought about how we used to play cards together—go fish and crazy eights and hearts—and how he used to let me win. I always wanted him to play his hardest so my wins would be real wins, so I could know I was good enough to beat him. But that wasn't what I remembered most. It was being on the couch next to him with his knee touching mine, and his big, warm hand on my back when I won.

If I closed my eyes I could still feel it. The warmth of it.

Ape Face knocked on my door after I was already in bed. "Isabelle?" she said. "Can I come in?"

"What do you want?" I said quietly, as if Mom was asleep, which I knew she wasn't.

I was hoping Ape Face would say "Never mind. Forget it," and go away. The thing with Ape Face is she never does. She's like a homing pigeon that keeps coming back even when you're mean to her. Maybe if she were my older sister I wouldn't mind so much, I'd like having her around. I could talk to her about things. But what are you going to talk about with Ape Face? She's only ten. It's not like she understands anything about anything.

The voice on the other side of the door said, "Please, Isabelle?"

"Fine," I said. "But only for a minute."

I turned on the radio next to my bed, very softly. WKLB, the New Country 99.5, the same station Aunt Weezy plays in her car.

I moved over so Ape Face could sit down on the bed.

"Isabelle?" she said. "What's wrong with Mom?"

"What are you talking about? Nothing's wrong with Mom."

"Listen," said Ape Face. "Do you hear that? She's like, moaning. Hear it?"

I sighed. "She's not moaning. She's crying."

"Why?"

"Come on, April. Why do you think? Because her pet squirrel has the measles."

"What? Mom has a pet squirrel?"

I made a sound in the back of my throat. Sometimes ten-year-olds are so dense you want to shove them off the bed.

Ape Face looked straight at me then. "Because of Daddy. Right? . . . Right, Isabelle?"

I nodded.

We were quiet for a minute. Ape Face grabbed the edge of my blanket and rubbed the silky part between her fingers. "It scares me when she cries," she said.

"I know."

"Isabelle? You don't think she's going to . . . you know . . . like Jenny Singer's mom?"

"What? Kill herself? No way."

"But Margot Reilly said that Jenny Singer's mom— "

"Listen, Ape Face. There's no way that's going to happen. So just shut up about it. Just *shut up*."

Ape Face shut up for about two seconds. Then she said, "Can I sleep in here with you tonight, Isabelle? Just for tonight?"

"No way!"

Ape Face stood up right away. She started walking toward the door.

"Listen, Ape," I said. "Just put a pillow on either side of your head, like a sandwich, and hum for a while. It helps."

After Ape Face left, I made my own pillow sandwich, clasping my arms around my head. I thought about the look on my little sister's face when I told her no way could she sleep with me, like I slapped her. A good big sister would say "Sure, April, no problem," and rub her back until she fell asleep. A good big sister would help her with her stupid family tree project. I might as well do that, seeing as I'm pretty good at projects. You can buy colored poster board at the Save More for fifteen cents a piece. I could get her a purple piece. Purple is Ape Face's favorite color. She's absolutely bonkers about it.

 **17**

AFTER SCHOOL ON FRIDAY I was lying on Ashley's big white bed. It is so soft you sink into it like you're lying on a cloud. There's even a canopy, white with tiny blue flowers. And about five hundred fluffy white pillows. When you lie down you never want to get up again.

"So," Ashley said. "What do you want to eat?"

I opened my eyes. "I don't know. Anything, I guess."

"Ravioli? And chocolate chip ice cream? Waffles?"

"Sure. Whatever you want."

Ashley started getting excited. "I know! I can make

Belgian waffles! With ice cream and whipped cream and chocolate sauce and everything, and nuts—no! Nuts would be gross. Unless you want nuts, Isabelle?"

"No nuts."

Ashley smiled. "Right. No nuts. . . . And Diet Coke, right? With a twist. Like always."

"Like always."

"'Kay. I'll be back in like ten minutes or so."

"'Kay."

After Ashley left, I climbed down off the cloud bed and walked around her room. I walked through her closet packed with clothes hanging on silky padded hangers and thought, *How does she ever decide what to wear?*

I looked at myself in Ashley's white shell mirror and said out loud, "Whatever shall I wear today?"

I opened the top drawer of her bureau, which I assumed would be the underwear drawer, and it was. One pile for cotton. One pile for silky. I thought, *Holes and stains are not welcome here.*

I looked in the shell mirror again and said, "Hi. I'm Ashley. Ashley Barnum. Even my underwear is perfect."

The girl in the mirror snorted. "Ha! You're Belly. *Belly.*"

For a moment I thought I heard Ashley in the hall and I froze. But my watch said she'd only been gone two minutes.

Ashley's desk was very organized, everything in its place. I opened the top drawer. Pencils, all in a line, sharpened into perfect points. When I opened the second drawer it was filled with folded pieces of paper, wrapped together in bundles with rubber bands. On top of each bundle was a sticky with Ashley's writing on it. Notes from Ryan James. Notes from Jason Gullo. Notes from Dan Fosse. Notes from Peter Marsh. Notes from Brian King. Me, I would be happy with one note from a boy. One! More proof of how Ashley is the luckiest person ever.

I looked at my watch. I had time for one more drawer. I thought, *What could possibly be inside drawer number three, a million dollars? A party invitation from the President of the United States?* Instead, opening drawer number three was like taking a drink of what you think is going to be orange soda but turns out to be grapefruit juice. It was full of Cliffs Notes, and the top one was for *A Separate Peace*, the book we're reading in English. Certain pages were marked with paper clips.

I tried to remember what Mr. Minx told us at the beginning of the year: "Cliffs Notes are for cheaters. If you use Cliffs Notes you are not only cheating the system, you are cheating yourselves."

I thought to myself, *Ashley Barnum is a cheater.* I closed the drawer and ran back to the cloud bed. I dove headfirst into the fluff and felt my heart beating like crazy. Ashley Barnum is a cheater!

When Ashley came back she was the same as always. Big smile, not a care in the world. I sat on the bed cross-legged and watched her while she put the food tray down on the rug and laid out napkins.

She looked up at me. "What?"

"Nothing," I said. Because what else was I going to say? *So, anyway, I was snooping through your stuff. And I found your Cliffs Notes.*

Ashley said, "Hungry?"

I didn't know if I was hungry or not, but I nodded. "Smells good," I said.

She said, "Let's eat."

After we'd been shoveling food in for a while, Ashley stopped eating and wiped her mouth with a square of napkin. "If my mother saw me right now she'd kill me."

I swallowed a mouthful of ice cream. "How come?"

"Are you kidding me? Have you seen my mother eat? It's nothing but celery sticks and cottage cheese all day."

What I was thinking was, *How could I see your mother eat? Your mother's never home.* What I said was, "She must get hungry."

Ashley shrugged. She picked up a waffle and folded it in half before she stuffed it in her mouth. A glob of chocolate sauce stuck to her upper lip like a mustache. She swallowed the last of the Diet Coke in her glass. "Come on," she said. "If we wait too long we won't be able to get it all out."

I stood up and followed Ashley down the hall to the bathroom where there are two sinks right next to each other. We stuck our fingers down our throats at the same time. You wouldn't believe how fast and bubbly everything comes up if you drink a lot of Diet Coke first.

The whole time we were doing it I was thinking about what Trish said. Making yourself throw up is a sign that something else is wrong.

When we were finished we cleaned out the sinks with cleanser and sprayed peach air freshener all over.

"I feel so much better," Ashley said. "Don't you, Isabelle?

My head nodded yes, but other parts of me were saying *No!* Like my throat, which hurt. And my eyes, which wouldn't stop watering.

"I feel great!" Ashley said, rinsing her hands in the sink, rubbing a blob of toothpaste over her teeth.

She feels great. Great! I took a quick look at Ashley's face to see what I could see. Her mouth was smiling, all right.

The thing is, if you just look at a person's mouth you can be fooled. What you have to do is look at their eyes. That's where the truth is. And with Ashley, the eyes weren't saying *Great!*, I can tell you that.

 18

THE NEXT MORNING, WHEN I GOT HOME from Ashley's, Aunt Weezy was there. She and my mother were sitting at the kitchen table drinking coffee. They were dressed alike, cardigans over khakis, except Weezy had on her little drop earrings.

My mother was even wearing makeup. Mascara, blush, and pink lipstick—bright pink, like some pushy saleslady got her to buy it. Her hair was smoothed back into a head-band, lavender, to match her sweater.

For a second I thought maybe I'd walked into someone

else's house, but there was Ape Face in her pj's, slurping on a bowl of Cheerios. When she saw me she waved with her spoon, sending a spray of milk through the air.

My mother waved too, as though it was the most natural thing in the world for her to be up early on a Saturday morning, drinking coffee, dressed as Weezy's clone.

Weezy smiled and said, "Good morning, Isabelle."

I looked from my mother to Weezy and back again. "Good morning," I said.

My mother said, "Are you hungry, sweetie? We've got bagels."

"Okay," I said, and went on to butter myself a poppy seed bagel, because actually I was starving.

At Ashley's house, she made a gigantic breakfast, enough for the whole eighth grade, but I didn't feel like eating. When I looked at it, all I could think about was that we would have to throw it up after. I told Ashley I had to be home early, I didn't have time to eat.

I could tell she was upset, but she pretended not to be.

"I'm really sorry I can't stay, Ashley," I said. "I would if I could. It's just that I promised I'd be home by—"

"That's okay, Isabelle." Ashley smiled and shook her head like it was no big deal. "My brothers will be up soon," she said. "They'll be hungry."

But I knew that after I left she would eat it all herself.

I was glad to be here in my own kitchen, eating a bagel.

Ape Face said, "Doesn't Mom look pretty, Isabelle?"

I swallowed a big bite. "Uh-huh." To my mother I said, "Why are you all dressed up?"

Weezy reached over to pour her clone more coffee.

"Your mother and I are going out," she said, "for some quality sister time."

I thought, *quality* and *sister* should not be used together in the same sentence.

My mother said, "You don't mind holding down the fort, do you Isabelle? Looking after your sister?"

I took another bite of bagel, shrugged.

Ape Face said, "I don't need looking after."

I said, "I don't think I'm strong enough to actually *hold down* the fort. This is one big fort we've got here. This fort is—"

Aunt Weezy leaned over and pinched my arm, gently.

"Okay," I said.

Aunt Weezy patted my hand, smiled.

Me and Ape Face sitting at the kitchen table. Quality sister time.

"Mom looked weird," I said, "with all that makeup on. Like a clown."

"I think she looked nice," said Ape Face.

"You would."

"Aunt Weezy did it all. The clothes and the makeup, everything. She did her hair. Didn't her hair look nice, Belle?"

"It looked like a helmet."

Ape Face snickered. "It kind of did."

"I know."

Ape Face bent over and picked a Cheerio up off the table with her tongue, like a lizard. She does things like that, gross things. Like flipping her eyelids inside out and burping the alphabet. Things that make you want to smack a person upside the head. "I'm glad she's going out though," Ape Face said. "Maybe she'll come home happy."

"Right," I said.

I watched Ape Face tongue another Cheerio, chew it with her mouth wide open. Before she could do it a third time I picked up all the strays on the table and threw them in a bowl.

"Hey!" she said.

"Hay is for horses, but grass is much cheaper. You want help with your stupid family tree project or what?"

Finding the photos was easy. We just looked under her bed, in a big cardboard box marked "Jacob." If she didn't want us to find them, it wasn't a very good hiding place.

"Well," said Ape Face, "I guess she didn't throw them out after all."

We took off our shoes, climbed up on Mom's bed, which was made for a change, with clean sheets. Probably Aunt Weezy did that.

Right away Ape Face reached into the box and started yanking out clumps of photos with both hands.

"Don't!" I said. "You'll mess them up!" I wanted us to take our time, look at each picture together. Slowly. When a person dies and you suddenly find his pictures, that's how it is.

"Sorry," said Ape Face. "I just want to see them so bad."

"You think I don't?" I pulled the box toward me. "Let's do them one at a time."

"Okay." Ape Face moved over next to me so our

elbows were touching, which would usually bug me but didn't for some reason.

We both sat so still, barely breathing, looking at every photo. Mom and Daddy on the beach, tan and smiling, holding umbrella drinks. Daddy on the ski slopes, goofy in goggles. The four of us Lees eating hot dogs in the backyard.

When we got to the bottom of the pile, the last photo, Ape Face leaned over and put her chin on my shoulder. "I miss him, Isabelle. I still do, so much." Then, suddenly, she pulled away. "Do you?"

"Of course!" I said. "God, April!"

"I know. It's just sometimes, you know, I don't know. We never talk about him, so I think I'm the only one."

"Well, you're not."

We both got quiet for a second, looking down at the pictures all spread out.

April picked one up—Daddy and Mom dancing—and held it in her lap. "Do you cry ever?"

"Yes!"

"You do? When?"

"I don't know. When . . . in my room and stuff, when I'm alone. At night mostly."

"Really? Me too." She put her hand on my knee. "At night in my room."

"Mom too." I started laughing then, not because it was funny but because it was so stupid. "You cry in your room. I cry in my room. Mom cries in Mom's room. And in the morning everyone pretends like they never cried once in their life. Like, 'It's gonna be a great day, kids! Pass the orange juice!'"

"I know!"

April put the picture back in the pile. Then she bounced up off the bed. "Come on, Isabelle. We have to go."

"Go where?"

"Go get poster board and glue sticks and stuff. And some stickers. And . . . you know, those markers that smell like fruit."

"Okay, but I already got you poster board."

"You did?"

"Uh-huh. Two pieces, in case you mess up. Purple."

"You *did? Purple?*"

"Uh-huh. It's in my closet."

"You're the best sister, Isabelle. Seriously."

"Well," I said. "Not the best."

"Okay. Maybe not the best, but close."

Mom walked in the door carrying two bags of groceries. "Oh, Isabelle. You already made dinner. Thank you."

I told her it wasn't me, it was her other daughter. Yessiree, we were in for a real treat. Spaghetti à la Ape Face.

I ran upstairs to Project Central. "Listen," I said, "Mom's home. Put that somewhere she won't see it, quick."

Ape Face slid the photos and poster board under her bed.

In the kitchen, Mom was pouring milk into glasses, which seemed to match with her Aunt Weezy outfit. What didn't match was her face, pale and pinched looking.

She turned on the smile for dinner though, as usual.

"How was your day? No fighting, no biting, I hope."

"No fighting, no biting," said Ape Face. "Right, Isabelle?"

"Right," I said. Almost the truth, if you don't count the two swears I called her and the glue stick she threw at my head. This is what happens when Ape Face refuses to use a pencil and starts right in with the markers like an idiot. Lucky for her I bought two pieces of poster board.

"How was your day?" I asked my mother.

"Nice."

"Nice?" said Ape Face. "That's it?"

"No, it was . . ." Mom twirled a forkful of spaghetti, set it down again. "It was lovely. I guess I'm just tired from all the walking around we did." She looked at us and smiled. "I'm fine though."

I so much did not want to hear the words *tired* or *fine* anymore. My mother needed to come up with some new words for her vocabulary. Preferably some that weren't lies.

I wanted to scream at her, but I managed to keep my voice calm. "Mom," I said, "April and I were talking, and we really want to celebrate Hanukkah this year. It's been two years since we celebrated, and we miss it."

My mother picked up a napkin off the table and folded it in half. Then in quarters. Then in eighths.

"Mom?" I said.

She continued busily folding until there was nothing left to fold, until it was just a tiny napkin stub. Then she picked up another napkin.

"Mom?" April said.

"Yes."

"Can we do it?"

My mother stopped folding and looked at April. Then at me. Then said, "I don't think so. No. Not this year."

"But Mom," said April.

"Why not?" I said. "Give us one good reason. And don't tell us you're too *tired* to have this conversation because it has nothing to do with *tired*. And don't say we'll do it next year because we won't."

She stood up, still holding the second napkin. "I can't do it, girls. It's that simple. . . . I just . . . can't do it."

"You don't have to," I said. "We'll do it. Me and April. We'll do the whole thing."

"Yeah," said April. "You won't have to lift a finger. You can just show up and eat latkes."

We watched Mom's face getting red, her eyes start to water. "That's not the point," she said. "I'm sorry, girls. No. The answer is no." She pressed the napkin to one wet eye, then the other.

Under the table, April nudged me. I nudged her back, not to push her away, but to let her know I was glad she was there.

19

TRISH WANTS US TO JOURNAL constantly. If she had her way we'd be journaling every hour on the hour, until our hands cramped up into claws. Until our eyeballs popped out.

At first, journaling was the opposite of what I wanted to do, it was like torture staring at all that blank space. But then I started carrying my journal around with me to school like one of my regular notebooks, just in case the mood struck. And then, this one day, I wrote something. Perched on the toilet seat in a girls' bathroom stall.

What happened was I had lunch at Ashley's table for a bunch of days. The first couple of times I sat there I could feel Nola and Georgie's eyes boring into me the whole time, curious. And Paula's, jealous. But after a few days they stopped looking over, like they'd forgotten all about me. Which was okay because I had all these new friends. I sure did. Maya and Arielle and Jessie and Hannah and Heather and Talia and Sasha and Eliza. And, of course, Ashley. And I was having a wonderful time. I sure was. I was surrounded by the most popular girls in school, who wore all the right clothes and said all the right things and got invited to all the right places. And of course they were thinking, *Thank goodness Ashley introduced us to Isabelle, because now our little family is complete.*

But no. It wasn't that way at all. Not even close. It didn't matter how much Ashley Barnum liked me, I still didn't cut it. I was like a troll at a Barbie picnic.

Every day I ate at the center table I would run to the girls' room after lunch and throw up. But one time I sat there for a while thinking about what Trish is always saying to us. "Before you throw up, HALT. Ask yourself, how are you feeling? Are you hungry? Angry? Lonely? Or tired?"

And for once I took the pencil out of my mouth, wiped the spit off on my jeans, and wrote something. I wrote one word. Lonely.

Then, when the bell rang, I closed my journal and ruined everything by puking anyway.

"What makes you think you ruined everything?" Trish asked.

It was Tuesday again, four o'clock. The difference between this time and last time was I started talking the minute I sat down. I told Trish all about Ashley and the center table. Only I gave Ashley a code name. Penelope Lutz, after this girl I knew from nursery school, who moved to Oregon. Plus, I brought my journal, which actually had some writing in it now. In a way, I regretted bringing it. I didn't want Trish to get excited over nothing.

"Isabelle?"

"Yeah?"

"You said you 'ruined everything' by throwing up. What did you mean by that?"

"Like you told us. You want us to journal when we feel HALT feelings, right? Instead of throwing up, we should journal, you said. Right?"

Trish nodded.

"Well, I did. I wrote something. But then I still made myself throw up anyway, so what was the point?"

"Well. How did you feel while you were writing?"

"Okay . . . I guess."

"You felt okay."

"Yeah."

"And after?"

"After I journaled or after I barfed?"

"After you journaled. Did you feel better?"

"I don't know. I guess so. Yeah."

"All right, then," Trish said. "I would call that progress."

"Progress?"

"Yes."

"Even though I threw up anyway?"

Trish nodded. "Even though you threw up anyway. The progress, Isabelle, shows in your decision to try something else first. You were feeling badly, and what did you do? You wrote in your journal. You put your feelings on paper. Okay, so you threw up afterward. But next time, maybe you won't. Next time, maybe the writing will be enough."

I thought about this, then said, "What if it isn't?"

"If it isn't, we'll try something different."

I leaned back in my chair, rocked a little. I looked at Trish and thought, We. We'll try something different. Me and Trish.

"Bingeing and purging is not an easy cycle to break, Isabelle. Changing those habits, those deeply ingrained ways of dealing with your emotions, doesn't happen overnight. It takes practice and patience and hard work. But you can do it, and I can help you. Are you willing to let me?"

I looked at Trish. Her crazy red hair barretted back on two sides, like a little kid's. Her eyes on mine, waiting.

"Yeah."

Trish smiled. "Okay then."

I took a minute to picture myself, helped. Me, Isabelle Lee, a regular person eating regular meals and not throwing them up afterward. Not sitting on the floor of my closet stuffing Doritos down my throat, or sneaking down the stairs in the middle of the night to raid the refrigerator. Not having to cover my ears with a pillow sandwich and hum all the time.

Trish said, "What about your friend Penelope?"

"Who?"

"Your friend Penelope. Lutz, is it? From the center table. Tell me about her."

Ah yes, my good friend Penelope Lutz. "What can I say . . . she's perfect."

"Perfect?"

"Uh-huh. She's got the hair, the body, the clothes. Everything. Boys drooling all over her. A million friends. You know. Smart. At least I *think* she's smart. I used to think so, until . . ."

"Until?" Trish said.

I pretended to be very interested in the toothpaste splotch on my shirt. I frowned and picked at it with my fingernail. How could I tell Trish about the Cliffs Notes without telling her about me snooping? Which was worse, a cheater or a snoop?

"Isabelle?"

"She's just . . . trust me, okay? She's perfect. She's, like, the person everyone wants to be friends with."

Trish nodded. "She sounds great."

"Uh-huh."

Trish was quiet for a minute. Then, "Isabelle?"

"Yeah."

"Have you ever heard of something called the halo effect?"

I shook my head.

"I want you to read something." Trish stood up and walked over to a bookshelf filled with books. She picked out a fat blue one, flipped through it until she found what she was looking for. "Here. Page 172."

Trish put the book down on the desk, slid it toward me. She tapped the spot with her finger. "Start here."

I leaned in and squinted at the tiny writing. *The halo effect occurs when major character traits influence the overall impression, leading perceivers to infer trait information beyond what is actually given—*

"Is this English?" I asked.

Trish smiled. "Keep reading. I'll translate in a minute."

Attractive people are usually viewed as more socially capable, more influential, adjusted, and intelligent. The effect of attractiveness—"what is beautiful is good"—may be attributed to the halo effect.

I looked up. "Whatever that means."

"What it means is that people who are good-looking, people who are beautiful like your friend Penelope, are often perceived as being perfect simply *because* they are beautiful. We're so blinded by the prettiness, we don't see the imperfections. We don't see them as real people, with real flaws. In fact, we see them as smarter, nicer . . . cooler than the average person."

"Huh," I said.

Later that night, I thought about it. The halo effect. I pictured Ashley floating through the halls of school with her little gold halo on, everyone staring at her, thinking she was so great, that she had this great life.

Then I thought about the other things I knew about her. How she thought she was so fat even though she wasn't, how she made herself throw up all the time, and used Ex-Lax, and how her parents were hardly ever home. I remembered what Ashley said in Group that one time, about the girls in the magazines. "You can't always tell, just from looking."

At first I thought about calling her. I started to. But then I didn't. I lay in bed for a long time, wondering what it was really like to be Ashley Barnum.

**20**

AUNT WEEZY SHOWED UP AGAIN on Saturday morning, early, when I was the only one up. She was wearing a lime green cardigan and carrying a loaf of banana bread wrapped in cellophane. Instead of the drop earrings, she had on tiny pearl studs.

She followed me into the kitchen and I found a platter for the banana bread. She took a knife out of the silverware drawer and started slicing. "So. How are you doing, honey?"

I took a glass out of the cupboard, poured myself some juice. "Okay."

Weezy lowered her voice. "Your meetings? With the counselor? Are they helping?"

I nodded, picked up the juice and swirled it. "Kind of. Yeah."

"Good." Weezy took a breath, nodded. "Good. . . . So, I've gotten the name of a therapist, a grief counselor. And I've gone ahead and made your mom an appointment for next week."

"Aunt Weezy," I said. "No offense, but she's going to *freak*. She'll be so mad."

Weezy put the knife down and started arranging banana bread into the shape of a fan. "I know. But I have to do something. I can't just stand by pretending everything's fine."

I leaned my hip against the counter, whispered, "That's what she does. Pretends everything's fine all the time. Even though it isn't."

"I know it isn't, sweetheart. That's why I'm here." Weezy turned and looked at me, put a sticky hand on my arm. "I'm sorry I didn't know sooner, Isabelle. I just didn't realize."

"No. It's okay."

She nodded. "It will be. I can promise you that."

After Aunt Weezy and Mom left the house, April and I sat on the floor of her room and put the finishing touches on her family tree project. The pictures, color copies we made of the photos we found under Mom's bed, looked just like the real thing. We stared and stared at each one, at our dad smiling back at us like it was yesterday.

The letters of the title were rainbow. When you leaned in you smelled a fruit bowl. *The Lee Family Since 1922*.

Everything was crooked because Ape Face refused to use a ruler. That part killed me. No matter how many times I told her, she wouldn't listen. With Ape Face it's her way or the highway. You never met someone so stubborn in your whole life.

The rest looked great, though, I have to say. Especially the silver glitter for the tree, and the tiny gold stars for each year. You wanted to stop and read every branch, take your time and really get to know people. *Jacob Joshua Lee. Born June 11, 1961, Brooklyn, New York. Third Baseman, Brooklyn Rockets, 1976–1979. Graphic Artist, Cartoonist, Song Lyricist. Bilingual in French. Married Elizabeth Jayne Lawrence, 1984, on Squam Lake in New Hampshire.* It went on and on. Luckily, Ape Face actually listened to me for once and typed those parts on the computer, so the writing was perfect. If she didn't get an A-minus at least, her teacher was crazy.

"It's good, huh, Isabelle?"

"Yeah," I said. "It really is."

"Okay, so . . ." April leaned over, blew some stray glitter off the poster board onto the rug. "When do we show it to Mom?"

"I don't know. I've been thinking about that."

"And?"

"And I don't think we should show her yet. I think we should wait. Do it in a special way."

"Like how?"

I smiled just a little, careful to cover my teeth with my lips like the famous lady in the painting. Mysterious. Sometimes when you have a great idea you want to keep it to yourself for a while. You want to take your time with it.

21

ON WEDNESDAY, ASHLEY WASN'T in school. At lunch I stood in the doorway of the cafeteria with my brown bag, not knowing what to do. Then I started walking. At the center table was the usual gang, all of Ashley's friends. Whispering, giggling, tossing their hair . . . not waving me over. Right. I walked past them, holding my breath, looking straight ahead.

Nola and Georgie would understand, I knew they would. They had to. So, I hadn't sat with them for two weeks. So, people make mistakes, right? First, I'd explain it to them. Then they'd forgive me. Then we'd all say we're sorry. Then I could sit down and it would be just like I never left.

After I walked around the cafeteria twice, I started feeling a little panicky, light-headed. Trish would say I was breathing too fast. Take slow deep breaths, she would tell me. In through your nose, out through your mouth.

My third lap through the cafeteria. In through my nose. Out through my mouth. What was the matter with me? Why couldn't I just do it? Why was it the only thing I wanted to do was run to the bathroom and lock myself in the stall? Stuff my lunch down my throat and . . .

But then, I did it. I took one more deep breath and walked straight over to Nola and Georgie's table. I decided to try the jokey approach. "Pardon me," I said. "Is this seat taken?"

No one laughed.

Georgie pretended she hadn't heard me. Paula kept right on eating potato chips. So I focused on Nola. She was the one who hated fighting the most.

"Nola!" I said, holding my lunch bag in front of me like a purse. "Can I sit with you guys?"

Nola picked up her sandwich, peanut butter on pumpernickel as usual. She took a careful bite, then set the sandwich down on a napkin. She chewed, swallowed, and looked at me. Finally she said, "Why do you want to sit with us again, Isabelle?"

And I said, "I don't know. I guess I like it better over here."

Nola picked up her chocolate milk and shrugged. "Fine with me."

Georgie was tougher. "Nobody likes a fair-weather friend, Isabelle. Make a decision and stick with it."

I thought about Ashley for a second. What would she think when she came back to school and I wasn't sitting at her table anymore? She had so many friends, would she even notice?

I looked Georgie in the eye. "This is my decision," I told her, meaning it. "I want to sit with you guys."

"Whatever," Georgie said. "Do what you want."

I did what I wanted. I sat down.

When Paula asked what it was like sitting at the center table, I thought hard before I answered. "It was like . . . getting invited to a Halloween party that you're really excited about. Only, when you show up at the door, you're the only one wearing a costume."

Nola set down her milk carton. "It's a Halloween party. Why wouldn't you wear a costume?"

"Exactly."

"Where were you today?" I said.

It was Group, and here was Ashley sitting across from me. Trish had us doing another mirroring exercise and we were partners again, just like we were back before we knew each other. Being Ashley's mirror is different when you know her. You don't see her as some big mystery anymore. And in a way, you wish she still was. You want to keep on believing she's this perfect person without a care in the world.

"Why weren't you in school?" I said again. "Were you sick?"

Ashley looked down, twisted a button on her shirt. "Yeah. I wasn't feeling great this morning." She looked up and smiled. "But I'm feeling better now. Thanks."

"Sure," I said. I didn't want her to think I didn't believe her. But really, Ashley sounded just like my mother. *I'm fine. Really. Everything's fine.*

On our way out of Group, Ashley grabbed my hand. "Isabelle. Want to go out to dinner or something? I've got money. We can go anywhere you want."

"I can't," I said. "I have to be home. I told my sister I'd help her cook."

"Oh." Ashley tried to smile but didn't quite make it. "Okay."

I said, "Aren't your parents expecting you for dinner?"

Ashley shook her head. "My mom's away on her spa week. In California. And my dad's working on this really big case. He won't be home until late."

"What about your brothers?" I asked.

"I don't know. You never know with them."

"So, no one's home at your house?"

Ashley shook her head. "Except for Gregory."

"Gregory the cook?"

"Yeah."

"Well," I said, "you like mini pizzas?"

Ashley nodded, tried to smile again.

"Good," I said. I pulled her arm. "That's what we're making."

Ape Face was definitely impressed, Ashley being about the coolest person she'd ever met in her life. She wanted to be just like her, immediately, which didn't surprise me one bit.

"You play field hockey?" said Ape Face. "Me too! Only in gym, but still. I'm pretty good except for my scoop pass, which pretty much rots."

Ashley knew exactly how to reel her in. "I could help you some time. If you wanted."

"No way! Really, Ashley? *Really?* That would be so cool."

It was me and Ape Face and Ashley, all sitting around the kitchen table, rolling out pizza dough. Spreading tomato sauce and sprinkling little shreds of cheese. You might think this would be weird, having Ashley Barnum at your house for the first time, but it isn't. Not when you know her.

The only thing I was worried about was my mother, who would be down any second, wearing any number of nutso personalities. I wanted her to act normal, not like she usually does, down and out, or super excited in that fake way.

"How do you get your hair like that, Ashley?" said Ape Face. "So shiny?"

"Come on, April," I said. "Enough questions already."

"It's okay, Isabelle," said Ashley. "I don't mind. You know what the trick is? Vinegar. A cool vinegar rinse after you shampoo."

"Really?" Ape Face said. "Vinegar?"

"Uh-huh."

My mother walked into the kitchen wearing jeans and a corduroy shirt. She looked not too bad. Pretty soon she was smiling and introducing herself to Ashley, like a regular mom would do.

"It's a pleasure to meet you, Ashley."

"You too, Mrs. Lee."

I watched my mother and Ashley smile and nod, take

each other in. I watched my mother fall in love at first sight. Because how could you not love Ashley Barnum? She was the perfect daughter.

"So, Ashley, how do you and Isabelle know each other?"

"From school," said Ashley. "We have the same English class."

"From *Group*," I said. "We have the same eating disorder."

When everyone turned to stare at me, I shrugged. "What? It's true."

Wasn't it time someone started telling the truth around here? Even if the truth stinks?

After dinner, my mother and Ape Face headed into the den to watch a movie so Ashley and I could have some time alone. This was my mother's idea, which meant she was actually paying attention for a change. Ape Face didn't like it, but she went along with it. Probably because she planned to barge in on us later.

Upstairs in my room, we sat on my bed, pj'd, washed, brushed.

"Your mom's so nice," Ashley said.

"You think?"

Ashley nodded. "Yeah. . . . You look alike."

I said, "No, we don't."

"Yes, you do. Your mouth or something." Ashley held up her hand to her lips and drew a little circle in the air. "Or your eyes."

I thought, *Oh yeah? You should see her eyes when she's not faking it for guests: red and puffy.*

"And April. What a cutie."

I nearly choked on my own spit. "I'm not sure *cutie* is the word."

Ashley paused. "Anyway. You're lucky."

Yeah, right, I thought. But I didn't say anything.

Ashley looked around the room, quiet for a second, then picked up a pillow and held it to her chest. "Why'd you tell them I'm in Group?"

"Because you are," I said. "I just don't see any point in lying."

Ashley sat hugging the pillow, fingers wrapped around her elbows. Her hair was pulled back in a lacey white headband that matched her nightgown. Even when you know her, you still can't help thinking she's so pretty it's ridiculous. You almost want to pinch her to make sure she's real.

"Why not?" Ashley said.

"Why not what?"

"Why not lie? Everyone does."

Ashley lay the pillow in her lap. She stroked it a couple of times like it was a cat. Then she flipped it over and stroked it some more. The cat routine was starting to get old.

"What do you mean?" I said, grabbing the pillow. "Like who?"

"Like . . ." Ashley looked away. "Well, like my dad."

I wasn't sure I wanted to hear anything about Ashley's dad. She had one, and she should feel lucky. Any dad is better than no dad.

"What?" I said, finally. "What does he lie about?"

Ashley looked up and you could see she was trying not

to cry. She was biting her lip like crazy, and her eyes were getting red around the edges.

"Okay," she said finally. "I'll tell you. You ready?"

I nodded.

"I think my dad has a girlfriend. I mean, I know he does. I heard my mom talking about it. He kept telling her nothing was going on, but then she found it out anyway."

I was stunned for a second. "What?" I said. "Are you sure?"

"Positive."

"No way."

"I know," she said. Then, "They're getting a divorce."

"Are you sure?"

"I'm sure."

I handed Ashley a tissue from the box next to my bed. She blew her nose, then held out her hand for another one. I kept handing her tissues until there was a big wet pile between us. I did what Trish says is the only thing anyone can do. I listened.

"So," Ashley said finally, after she'd blown her nose for the thousandth time. "That's why I wasn't in school today. I was helping my father pack. He's, like . . . gone."

"Oh, Ashley," I said. Because I didn't know what else to say.

At one in the morning, we were standing in my kitchen.

"Let's make popcorn," Ashley said, looking through the cabinet. "With lots of butter."

"I don't know. I don't think we should cook. We might wake up my mom."

"Well . . . cereal, then. Something."

We already ate peanut butter sandwiches. And Oreos. When we got to the leftover pizza, I wasn't hungry anymore, so I stopped eating. Ashley didn't even notice. "Do you have anything to drink? Diet Coke?" She ate so fast, I felt sick just watching her. I sat back in my chair, pushed my plate away.

"Or regular Coke," Ashley said. "Anything with bubbles."

I knew what she meant. Anything that would help her throw up easier.

"We don't have any soda," I said. "I'll get you some OJ."

I went to the fridge and opened the door. Behind me, I knew, Ashley had both hands in her mouth at the same time, stuffing the food down. I didn't want to watch her anymore.

"Never mind," Ashley said. Before I could give her the juice, she ran to the kitchen sink, leaned over, and threw up. She didn't even use her fingers. When she was done, she scrubbed everything with cleanser. Then she turned to me, wiping her mouth with the back of her hand. "Aren't you going to?"

I shook my head.

"You don't want to?"

"No," I said. "I don't."

I don't know who was more surprised, Ashley or me.

22

ON MY WAY TO MY MEETING with Trish, it hit me. That night at my house with Ashley was the first time I ever said no to her. I wasn't sure what this meant, but it felt big to me.

"What do *you* think it meant?" Trish said, when I asked her. Trish loves answering questions with questions.

"I don't know," I said. "I didn't really care what she thought, for once. Do you think?"

"Before that, you used to care? You wanted her to think well of you?"

"I guess so," I said. "Yeah."

Trish looked at me. "So it was a big deal that you made a different choice? The choice not to throw up?"

"Well," I said, looking down. "I didn't throw up with her. Later on I did, though. When I was by myself."

"And what were you feeling then, Isabelle? When you were by yourself. Can you put your finger on it?"

"I was thinking about . . . my dad. Missing him. I was . . . you know, sad."

"Good," Trish said.

I looked up. "*Good?*"

"Not good that you felt sad. Good that you're beginning to identify your feelings."

"But I still threw up," I said. "Isn't that . . . I mean, aren't I supposed to be not doing that?"

Trish nodded. "Ultimately. Yes. When you're ready. To get yourself there, though, you have to do the work."

"What work?" I said.

"Being honest with yourself," said Trish. "And with me. Identifying your feelings. Journaling. Talking it out."

"I'm doing that," I said. "I mean . . . aren't I?"

"You are."

"I am."

"Okay then." Trish smiled. "Let's keep plugging. Let's talk some more about your dad."

At eleven that night, I was dialing Aunt Weezy's phone number, hoping that she would be the one that answered and not Uncle Jack, or worse, Nini. I'd already started to call about fifty times, hanging up before the first ring. This time, though, I was going to do it. I was doing what Trish said to do. Take deep breaths. In through the nose, out through the mouth. It was a bit exhausting.

"Aunt Weezy?" I whispered. "It's me. Isabelle."

"Isabelle? Honey? Is that you? I can barely hear you."

I raised my voice a little. "Yeah. It's me."

"Is everything all right? Is it your mom?"

"No. No. Everything's fine."

I could hear the sigh on the other end, like this was a big relief. It's amazing how people will just believe you when you say "Everything's fine," like saying it makes it true.

"Well," I said, "as fine as it ever is. You know."

Aunt Weezy sighed again. "Right."

"Anyway," I said. Now that we were back on track. "The reason I'm calling is, I've got this idea. And I kind of need your help."

There was Aunt Weezy's ear, wide open, waiting.

After I got off the phone, instead of going to bed right away, I took out my journal. I was sleepy, but I wasn't ready to go to sleep. There's something about talking to a person like Trish, or Aunt Weezy, that makes you think. Your head fills up with things that most of the time you hardly ever talk about. Normally I would head for my closet, for my stash, and start stuffing my face. This time I wrote.

Just minutes before, when I stood in the hallway outside my mother's room listening to her cry, I got mad. *Stop crying!* I wanted to yell. *Stop crying every night and do something about it!*

I wrote about that. And about how I wanted my mother back the way she used to be. I wanted her to be the mom again, taking care of me and April, not the other way around. I wanted her to stop pretending that everything was fine when it wasn't. Mostly, I wanted her to know that she wasn't the only one who missed him. We all did. Because he was all of ours.

 **23**

THE FIRST NIGHT OF HANUKKAH fell on a Thursday. As soon as I got home from school I started getting things ready. Even though Aunt Weezy promised to make sure my mother was out of the house, I checked her bedroom. Just in case.

April did everything I asked her to without making a peep. But I still watched her every move like a hawk to make sure she didn't screw it up.

My stomach was full of the butterflies you feel when you see a guy like Eli Bronstein walking down the hall toward you, and you're thinking, *Oh no, is he going to talk to me? And if he does, what if I freeze? Or say something stupid? Or let out a big raunchy burp?*

I hoped we were doing the right thing, me and April. I thought we were at first, but all of sudden I wasn't sure.

"It looks good, Isabelle, huh?" April said, taking a step back from the dining room table. "I'm glad we decided to go with the blue candles, instead of plain white."

I sat folding napkins, over and over until I got them right. Cloth ones, not paper. And not your regular folds either. Swans.

"You know?" April said. "Aren't you glad we went with the blue?"

"Yeah. They look good."

"Everything looks just right. Huh, Isabelle?"

"Yes," I said, placing one napkin swan on each plate. "It really does."

"It really does."

I smiled at this, Ape Face repeating everything I say because she wants me to know she's with me. We're in it together.

"Should I go get the rest of the stuff now?" she asked. "From upstairs?"

"Yeah. You do that. I'll check on the food."

"Right. You check on the food." April started walking out of the room, then stopped and turned back. "Isabelle?"

"Yeah?"

"I think Daddy would really like this. That we're doing this, I mean. If he could see us right now. You know what I mean?"

I felt my eyes sting when she said that. I had to bite

my lip and swallow hard. "Yeah, April. I know what you mean."

Aunt Weezy was there with us when my mother walked in the room. "Hi, Bethy," she said softly. And then, "Happy Hanukkah."

My mother looked at Aunt Weezy. She looked at me. And April. And the table, the menorah, Daddy's chair with April's family tree project propped on top of it, the whole thing. You could see her eyes moving around like crazy.

"You can't be serious," she said.

At first, nobody said anything.

Then, I broke the silence. "Well. We are. So, Happy Hanukkah."

"Happy Hanukkah, Mommy," said April.

"Happy Hanukkah?" my mother said. *"Happy Hanuk-kah?"*

Now she turned and looked at Aunt Weezy again, as though she needed to talk to an adult about this. Aunt Weezy just nodded, gestured to the empty chair for her to sit down.

I was too busy watching my mother's face to care if she was standing or sitting. I knew she was going to lose it any second now. Which is exactly what she did.

"How could you let them do this, Louise? I can't do this! I can't!"

"Bethy," Aunt Weezy said quietly, walking toward my mother with her arms outstretched.

"No!" my mother said. "There's no reason to do this!

No reason!" And then, to me and April, "Why did you do this? I told you we weren't going to do this."

"Bethy," Aunt Weezy said again.

My mother didn't answer. She just turned and ran out of the room.

Aunt Weezy came around to our side of the table, giving each of us a quick hug. "Girls. Sit tight. I'll be right back."

Soon it was just me and April, alone again, and Ape Face was starting to ask a million questions. "Do you think she'll come back, Isabelle? Mom, I mean? Do you think she's really mad? . . . Maybe we shouldn't have done this, you know? After she said not to?"

I didn't answer.

"Do you think we should just, you know . . . start picking up?"

"No!" I said. I knew my voice sounded sharp, but I didn't care. "We're not picking up anything. It's Hanukkah, and we're going to have Hanukkah."

Ape Face did what a good sister should do in a situation like that: she shut up. She shut up and listened to directions.

Together we walked to the head of the table where the menorah was, and picked up the lead candle, the Shamash. April held the Shamash while I lit the match, then we placed it in its holder at the same time.

Just like we planned, I sang the first blessing, the one Daddy always did. "Baruch atah Adonai eloheinu melech ha-olam asher kideshanu b'mitzvotav v'tzivanu l'hadlik ner shel Hanukkah."

When it was April's turn, she looked scared. "I might mess up, okay, Isabelle? I'm not sure I remember the whole thing. I've been practicing, like you showed me, but I'm still not—"

"Just do the best you can," I said. "I'll help you if you get stuck. Okay?"

"Okay." April closed her eyes tight. "Baruch atah Adonai eloheinu melech ha-olam, sheh' asah nissim l'avoteinu, ba-yamim ha-heim, ba-z'man ha-zeh. . . . Was that right? I thought it sounded pretty good."

"It did," I said. "It was perfect."

"Thanks."

"You're welcome," I said. "Now. Aunt Weezy was supposed to do the third blessing, and I don't exactly remember it. Do you?"

April shook her head.

"Okay." I walked back over to my chair and picked up the prayer book we'd found under my mother's bed. It was our father's, from when he was a boy.

I turned to April. "God doesn't care if you don't have it memorized. Remember how Daddy used to say that?"

She smiled. "Yeah."

I walked back to the head of the table with the prayer book, turned to the third blessing. "On three, okay?"

"On three," April said.

"One, two, three . . ."

Even though we were singing from the book, not from memory, the words sounded warm and right filling the air. "Baruch atah Adonai, eloheinu melech ha-olam—"

For a split second, in the middle of the blessing, I

looked up. There they were in the doorway, my mother and Aunt Weezy, watching us. I sang louder. "Shehecheyanu, v'ki-y'manu, v'higiyanu, lazman hazeh!"

Then I did a crazy thing, in front of everyone. I turned to my father's chair, which was empty except for the family tree project leaning against it, and I raised my water glass. "Happy Hanukkah, Daddy."

Without my even glancing at her, April did the same thing. "Happy Hanukkah, Daddy."

Then Aunt Weezy. "Happy Hanukkah, Jacob. We miss you."

I turned to my mother, standing in the doorway. Tears running down her face, buckets of them. I watched as she walked slowly across the room and sat down at the table. She didn't say a word, but she didn't have to. It was all right there.

 24

FRIDAY WAS THE LAST DAY before winter break and school was a madhouse. Most of the teachers had just given up trying to teach and were showing movies instead. Not Minx, though. The minute we sat down, he handed out a new book.

"*To Kill a Mockingbird*," Minx said, "is one of the great American novels. A coming-of-age story with a moral epicenter. For those of you who are considering a career in the law . . ."

While Minx droned on and on, Georgie and I sat next to each other playing tic-tac-toe with pink nail polish.

Denise Miller drew pictures of Minx with horns and a tail and passed them around the room.

Peter Marsh and Dan Fosse made spitball shooters out of their ballpoint pens, firing at each other whenever Minx wasn't looking. Every five minutes, one of them would make a fart noise out of the side of their mouth, until Minx finally looked up, frowning. "What's going on here?"

Dan said, "I'm sorry, Mr. Minx. My mother made me a Mexican omelet for breakfast, and you know what happens when I have beans for breakfast—"

"Never *mind*," said Minx, and the whole class cracked up.

Too bad Ashley wasn't there to see it. The room seemed empty without her. Brian King was completely bummed. He'd written an extraspecial Ashley poem, for Christmas.

"I can send it to her, if you want," I told him. "I know where she's staying in Colorado."

But Bri said no, thanks. He'd put it in her locker, so she'd have something waiting for her when she got back.

Ashley left that morning for her ski trip. She stopped by my house before school, with presents.

"You didn't have to do this, Ashley," I said, standing out on the porch with her while her mom sat in the driveway in her big black car.

"I know I didn't have to," said Ashley. "I wanted to."

"But I don't have anything for you!"

"That's okay," she said. "I like giving presents better than getting them anyway. This one," Ashley handed me something small and square, wrapped in blue tissue, "this is for April. It's a new field hockey ball. The best kind. Don't tell her, though! I want her to be surprised."

"She'll love it," I said, meaning it.

"And this one's for your mom." She handed me a green rectangle, a book. "It's a journal. She's an English teacher, right? She must like to write."

I nodded.

"And this," Ashley said, holding out a tiny silver package with a gold ribbon, "this is for you. Open it later." She handed me a white envelope, a card. "When you're alone, okay?"

"Okay," I said. "Ash. You really didn't have to do all this."

She hugged me, hard. "I wanted to."

I hugged her back.

Ashley pulled away suddenly, glanced over at the car where her mom was sitting. "It feels strange. Without my dad."

"I know it does."

Ashley looked at me. "Oh, Isabelle. I'm so sorry. I can't believe I said that. I still have a dad, and you . . ."

I shook my head. "It's okay."

"No, it's not." Ashley looked down, then up again, right at me. "Here I am going on and on about my dad moving out, and—"

"It's okay. Really."

"Still. I'm really sorry."

"I know."

"No. I mean it. And if, when I get back, you want to talk, you call me. I mean it. 'Kay?"

"'Kay."

"Promise?"

"Yeah."

Ashley leaned in again, hugged me hard. "I'm really going to miss you."

"Hey," I said. "You're crushing the presents."

She pulled back, half laughing, half crying. "Merry Christmas, Isabelle." Then she turned and ran down the steps, to the car where her mom was waiting, before I could say a word.

It was the weirdest feeling, standing on the porch in my slippers, watching her go. Sadness and relief at the same time.

As the car pulled out of the driveway, I pictured Ashley on the slopes in Aspen, whizzing down the mountain in her ski outfit, something blue and shiny, with her hair flying out behind her. I pictured her in the lodge by a roaring fire, taking off her boots, while guys with tans and names like Biff and Lance fought over who got to rub her feet.

Maybe it was more realistic to picture her shoving down her fifth chocolate chip pancake, or throwing up in a sink somewhere, or crying and crying because her dad wasn't there with them, but that's not what I was picturing. That's not how I wanted it to be for her.

"Merry Christmas, Ash," I whispered. And walked back inside to get ready for school.

 25

EVEN THOUGH IT WAS VACATION, we had Group as usual. Me and Mathilde and Dawn and Lila and Rachel—who was back, still wearing a ton of black eyeliner but nicer to be around.

We sat in our circle, talking about Christmas. "It's supposed to be this really happy day," Mathilde said quietly, "but sometimes it's not. I mean, not in my house." And Dawn said, "Mine either."

The rest of us nodded.

Trish said, "All right. Good! Let's talk about it. What makes the holidays so hard?"

At that, Mathilde and Lila both started crying and Trish passed the tissues. Dawn walked around the circle, giving out hugs.

Everyone started talking then, one at a time. I sat quietly, listening to Mathilde tell us about eating all the Christmas cookies her mother made, dozens of them, and then lying about it, saying the dog did it. Rachel talked about her father drinking a whole bottle of scotch and passing out at the dinner table, right in the middle of the toast.

I listened to everyone's story, each one surprising and not. I had no idea their families were so messed up. And yet, it made sense that we were all here.

I was so quiet, the only one in the circle not talking.

"Isabelle?" Trish said, when everyone else had gone. "Anything you'd like to share?"

"No," I said. And then, feeling everyone's eyes on me, "I mean . . . give me a second."

"Take your time," Trish said gently. "We're in no rush."

I sat for a while with my eyes closed, just breathing. "Okay," I said finally. "It's a hard time of year in my house because . . . because my dad isn't here with us anymore. Because he died. And we all miss him so much we want to explode."

The words sounded so strange coming out of my mouth, like they belonged to somebody else. For a second I wanted to hide. But then I looked up at everyone and saw that they were looking right back at me, nodding. Getting it.

I reached my hand out for a tissue, as though holding one would help me talk better. And in a way, it did.

The next day I was back in the same room, talking to Trish. It was Christmas Eve and we weren't supposed to be meeting, but Trish changed her mind at the last minute and called me to come in. Apparently she was proud of me, for finally opening my mouth in Group, and she wanted to tell me so.

"How did it feel yesterday?" Trish asked. "Talking about your dad?"

"Not bad," I said. "Weird at first. Everyone was looking at me, you know? But then, after I got going, not bad."

"Let me tell you something, Isabelle. The more you talk, the easier it gets."

"Yeah?"

"Absolutely."

We sat quietly for a moment. Then I told Trish about Penelope Lutz. About how Penelope was really Ashley Barnum. From Group.

Trish nodded, like she wasn't all that surprised.

I went on, saying how Ashley had given me a Christmas present and how I hadn't opened it yet. And I wasn't sure I was going to.

Trish said, "Why not?"

I thought before I spoke. "I guess because . . . whatever is in the box could never be as good as what I imagine is in the box. You know?" I wasn't sure Trish would get what I meant, until I saw that she was nodding.

"You might be surprised, though," Trish said. "Pleasantly."

"I might," I said, thinking about it. "Maybe I'll read the card first, see what it says. Then decide."

Trish smiled, not telling me what to do either way. That's how it is with her, not pushing so much as making you think.

"How are things with your mom?" Trish asked.

Oh. Right. That. "I don't know. Better, I guess. I mean, at least we're starting to talk about him some. She still can't say his name without crying, but she doesn't run out of the room or anything. And she's seeing this person, this grief therapist guy that my aunt found for her. Once a week. So . . ."

"Oh, Isabelle. That's great news. That's really a step in the right direction."

"I guess. She still has a long way to go though. You know. She's still a mess."

Trish nodded, rocked a little in her chair. "And the bingeing and purging? How are you doing with that?"

This time I smiled. "Well. I didn't throw up at all yesterday. And I haven't thrown up yet today. So that's, let's see . . . twenty-four, thirty-two . . . thirty-five hours and counting."

Trish leaned forward, her eyes on mine. "Thirty-five hours? Isabelle!"

"And counting."

"Isabelle!" Trish said again. Then, softly, "That's wonderful."

When it was time to go, I stood in the doorway for a long time, looking around the room at everything, squinting at my old friend the yawning dog. "Trish?" I said finally. "How come this room always smells like Cheez-Its?"

Trish smiled, walked over to her desk, opened a drawer. There was a moment of crackling cellophane before she held up the Cheez-Its bag. "Stay for a snack?"

I laughed, shook my head. "No, thanks. I've got to get home. Mom and April are waiting for me."

You might think it's a crazy way to spend Christmas Eve, standing in the den with your mom and your sister, not hanging ornaments on a Christmas tree, but hanging pictures of your dead dad on the wall. You might think it's nuts, but it's not.

I am up on the ladder because I am the only one not afraid of falling. April's job is to hand me the hammer and the nails when I need them. Mom passes me the framed photos, one at a time. One at a time, up they go. The memories that used to live here.

Mom and Daddy on their wedding day, all shining eyes and white teeth. Daddy and me at a football game when I was three, me on his shoulders holding a baton. The four of us out on the porch in summer, April on Mom's lap and me on Daddy's, all making monkey faces. Best of all, the picture of Daddy in high school, wearing his baseball uniform, so handsome you can't believe you're related.

We're hanging some new ones too, ones Aunt Weezy took of the three of us. Me, Mom, and April, out in the backyard, all huddled together because it's cold. If you look close, you can see the first snowflakes of the season, just starting to fall.

April keeps telling me that I'm hanging the pictures crooked.

I grit my teeth and swallow hard. Instead of saying "Shut up, Ape Face," I say, "Just tell me which way to go."

Finally we have them all hung, straight and even and beautiful. We stand back and admire our work.

"It looks great," says April. "Huh, Mom? Huh, Isabelle? It looks really great, doesn't it?"

"Yeah," I say. "It really does."

At first my mother just stands there, nodding, looking awfully close to crying.

"Mom?" I say.

Then she leans over, kisses my forehead. She grabs April, kisses her forehead too.

I don't think she can talk right now, my mom. But that's okay. Maybe she'll talk later. For now, there's the three of us, holding each other up.

A freelance writer and camp director,
NATASHA FRIEND has taught at
the Brearley School in New York City
and Ecole Bilingue in Cambridge. She
lives in Massachusetts with her husband, Erik, and baby, Jack. *Perfect* is
her first novel.

Ten Steps to a Positive Body Image

One list cannot automatically tell you how to turn negative thoughts into a positive body image, but it can help you think about new ways of looking more healthfully and happily at yourself and your body.

1.   Appreciate all that your body can do. Every day your body carries you closer to your dreams. Celebrate all of the amazing things your body does for you—running, dancing, breathing, laughing, dreaming, etc.

2.   Keep a top-10 list of things you like about yourself—things that aren't related to how much you weigh or what you look like. Read your list often. Add to it as you become aware of more things you like about yourself.

3.   Remind yourself that "true beauty" is not simply skin deep. When you feel good about yourself and who you are, you carry yourself with a sense of confidence, self-acceptance, and openness that makes you beautiful regardless of whether you physically look like a supermodel. Beauty is a state of mind, not a state of your body.

4.   Look at yourself as a whole person. When you see yourself in a mirror or in your mind, choose not to focus on specific body parts. See yourself as you want others to see you—as a whole person.

5.   Surround yourself with positive people. It is easier to feel good about yourself and your body when you

are around others who are supportive and who recognize the importance of liking you just as you are.

6. Shut down those voices in your head that tell you your body is not "right" or that you are a "bad" person. You can overpower those negative thoughts with positive ones. The next time you start to tear yourself down, build yourself back up with a few quick affirmations that work for you.

7. Wear clothes that are comfortable and that make you feel good about your body. Work with your body, not against it.

8. Become critical of social and media messages. Pay attention to images, slogans, or attitudes that make you feel bad about yourself or your body. Protest these messages: Write a letter to the advertiser or talk back to the image or message.

9. Do something nice for yourself—something that lets your body know you appreciate it. Take a bubble bath, make time for a nap, or find a peaceful place outside to relax.

10. Use the time and energy that you might have spent worrying about food, calories, and your weight to do something to help others. Sometimes reaching out to other people can help you feel better about yourself and can make a positive change in our world.

What Are Eating Disorders?

Eating disorders are illnesses that cause people to change the way they eat, which can lead to serious physical and emotional problems. Anorexia Nervosa and Bulimia Nervosa are illnesses that can become very dangerous to a person's health.

Anorexia Nervosa is a disease in which a girl starves herself—losing so much weight that she can become very sick. She constantly worries about her weight and how her body looks. Boys and men can become anorexics, too, but it is much less common.

Bulimia Nervosa is an illness in which a person eats a large amount of food—called "bingeing"—and then often vomits. People with bulimia can also use laxatives, diet pills, or "water" pills to lose weight.

Eating disorders can lead to depression and drug and alcohol abuse. It is very important that a person gets help right away so she doesn't become very ill—making it harder to get well.

Here Are Some Warning Signs of Eating Disorders

Anorexia Nervosa
- Constantly thinking about food, your weight, and your body
- Starving yourself
- Constantly fearing gaining weight
- Not wanting to eat, except for tiny portions
- Saying you're not hungry when you really are
- Exercising too much

- Thinking you're fat when you're really skinny
- Feeling cold all of the time
- Losing your hair
- Not getting your period

Bulimia Nervosa
- Constantly thinking about food, your weight, and your body
- Eating large amounts of food, usually in secret
- Vomiting after bingeing on food
- Abusing laxatives, diet pills, or "water" pills
- Exercising too much
- Having an irregular period
- Experiencing depression
- Feeling shame and guilt
- Feeling bad about yourself
- Feeling negative about many parts of your life
- Wanting to be by yourself a lot of the time
- Having problems with your friends and your family
- Being a perfectionist

HELP IS JUST A PHONE CALL AWAY!

ANAD—the National Association of Anorexia Nervosa and Associated Disorders—sponsors a toll-free hotline—(847) 831-3438—open from 9:00 A.M. to 5:00 P.M. CST. An ANAD counselor will:
- Help answer your questions
- Give you names of therapists from across the country who have special training in eating disorders

- Help you and your parents find special hospital programs
- Help you find a free ANAD Support Group in your area
- Help you find an ANAD resource person in your area to offer a helping hand

All of ANAD's services are absolutely free.

ANAD—the National Association of Anorexia
Nervosa and Associated Disorders
P.O. Box 7
Highland Park, IL 60035
(847) 831-3438
E-mail: anad20@aol.com
Web site: www.anad.org

My name is: Isabelle Eliza Lee
Please call me: Isabelle
I am: 13 yrs. old
I am in: 8th
I am here b/c: that was "the deal"
My personal goal is: ???

ISABELLE LEE HAS A PROBLEM.

And it's not just her little sister, April (aka Ape Face), who has just ratted her out to their mother. It's not even Group, which she now attends once a week as part of "the deal" with her mother. The problem is, everything seems "fine" at home, but in fact Isabelle's family is still reeling from the death of her father. Isabelle's mother has taken all the pictures of him off the walls and cries herself to sleep every night. When April catches Isabelle in the bathroom forcing herself to throw up, Isabelle can't bribe her to stay quiet and ends up in "Eating Disorder and Body Image Therapy Group." Trapped in a room with no air circulation and orange carpet, Isabelle is amazed when Ashley Barnum, the prettiest, most popular girl in school—aka Royalty—walks through the door.

In a world where appearances are all that matter, coping takes some interesting and potentially harmful turns.

$3.99 US

ISBN 0-439-90013

1600015

TAX INCLUDED
$5.50

EAN

9 780439 900133